TIME CAPSULE

TIME
capsule

Short Stories
About Teenagers
Throughout the
Twentieth Century

Edited by Donald R. Gallo

Published by
Dell Laurel-Leaf
an imprint of
Random House Children's Books
a division of Random House, Inc.
1540 Broadway
New York, New York 10036

Visit us on the Web! www.randomhouse.com/teens

Educators and librarians, for a variety of teaching tools, visit us at
www.randomhouse.com/teachers

ISBN: 0-440-22819-0

RL: 6.0

Reprinted by arrangement with Delacorte Press

Printed in the United States of America

November 2001

10 9 8 7 6

OPM

For my good buddies Sara and Bill

CONTENTS

ACKNOWLEDGMENTS

For historical information, I am thankful for several publications from Dorling Kindersley: *Chronicle of America*, revised edition (1997); *In the Beginning: The Nearly Complete History of Almost Everything*, by Brian Delf and Richard Platt (1995); and *Junior Chronicle of the 20th Century*, by Simon Adams et al. (1997). Other sources that provided valuable facts are *Famous First Facts*, fifth edition, by Joseph Nathan Kane, Steven Anzovin, and Janet Podell (H. W. Wilson Company, 1997); *The People's Chronology: A Year-by-Year Record of Human Events from Prehistory to the Present*, revised edition, by James Trager (Holt, 1994); *The Peopling of America: A Timeline of Events That Helped Shape Our Nation*, third edition, by Allan S. Kullen (The Portfolio Project, 1994); and various issues of *Time* magazine from 1998.

My thanks also to my wife, CJ, as well as to Michelle Poploff, Katie Torpie, and Jen Weiss for their helpful editorial suggestions.

INTRODUCTION

The Turn of the Century

If a family member didn't wake you up this morning, chances are you woke up to music from your clock radio. Like many other students your age, you used the toilet in your bathroom before brushing your teeth with your electric toothbrush, and you took a quick shower with a deodorant soap. After drying off, you worked a touch of gel into your hair and blew it dry. You might have dressed in your favorite jeans and designer shirt, adding your favorite scent. Slipping into your expensive sneakers, you headed to the kitchen for breakfast.

There you might have poured a bowl of your favorite cereal and added milk before taking a few gulps of orange juice. Still a little hungry, you grabbed a bagel from the freezer and popped it in the microwave while you searched for the peanut butter.

Pretty average morning.

But suppose today is not a normal day. Pretend for a few minutes that you live somewhere on the East Coast and that instead of going to school today, you're going to Hollywood, California, to appear on a talk show about how today's teenagers view the world.

Last night you packed your hard-sided suitcase, so all you have to do now is throw a couple of paperbacks and your sunglasses into your backpack. You grab your Discman and a couple of CDs before heading out.

Aboard a 747, you are soon flying comfortably at thirty-six thousand feet, watching a popular new movie while you sip a can of Coke. Later, you consider whether or not to eat the previously frozen airline meal that came with plastic utensils. The Snickers bar on your tray is definitely a bonus.

In a mere six hours you land in Los Angeles, grab your suitcase from the carousel, and head to your motel in Hollywood. Along the way you note with relief the golden arches of McDonald's and the red roof of a Pizza Hut. Looking at your digital watch, you are shocked to see (having passed through three time zones) that it's just noon. You've crossed the entire country and it's only lunchtime!

A fantasy, surely. But all of these things are possible today.

One hundred years ago almost none of these things could have happened to anyone. In 1900 there were no clock radios, no radio music, no digital watches, and certainly no television, videos, compact discs, or even movies. There were no electric toothbrushes, no deodorant soaps, hair gel, or blow-dryers. Breakfast cereals didn't come in boxes; milk didn't come in plastic containers. Milk didn't even come in bottles yet! And frozen food wasn't available because there were no freezers; there weren't even refrigerators. Although Coca-Cola had been invented in 1886 as a remedy for headaches and hangovers and Pepsi-Cola was created in 1898, they were dispensed only at soda fountains in drugstores. There were no plastics, no aluminum cans, no foil. No microwave ovens. No Big Macs. No pizzas. There weren't even indoor toilets, much less hot showers or electricity, in most homes. Teens didn't have sneakers in 1900, or designer clothes, or Walkmans or Discmans.

In 1900 there were no video or computer games to play, no organized activities such as Boy Scouts and Girl Scouts, no Little League, no miniature golf, no Rollerblades, no snowboards. And there were no malls or fast-food places to hang out in. Getting from place to place wasn't even easy.

For transportation, horses were still used extensively at the turn of the century, although trolley cars and trains provided public transportation in and between major cities. Only fourteen thousand automobiles existed at the end of 1900, and there were almost no paved roads, though that would soon change. The first flight—by the Wright brothers—was still three years away. And it wasn't until 1957 that jet planes began to carry paying passengers.

Back in 1900 you could have traveled to California from New Jersey, but it would have been by train, and you probably could not have gone alone. The journey would have taken days instead of hours, longer if your train went through Wyoming and was held up by the Wild Bunch. Headed by Butch Cassidy and the Sundance Kid, that gang was still robbing banks and trains in 1900.

One of the few things you own now that you could have owned in 1900 is jeans. Levi Strauss made the first denim jeans in San Francisco way back in 1850 for laborers. Back then, most younger teenage boys would have worn knickers with knee socks, and girls would have worn only dresses or skirts, never pants. Clearly, a lot has changed in a hundred years.

At the beginning of 1900, only ten years had passed since the last major encounter between the American military and the last free-roaming Native Americans (when 500 heavily armed soldiers of the Seventh Cavalry slaughtered more than half of the 350 mostly unarmed Sioux men, women, and children at Wounded Knee, South Dakota).

The average American at that time lived to age forty-seven; by 1998, the average life span was seventy-six. This remarkable increase would not have been possible were it not for important medical advances such as penicillin, antibiotics, cancer treatments, organ transplants, and artificial hearts. Polio and smallpox have been virtually eliminated, and tuberculosis and malaria have been greatly reduced. At the end of the century, AIDS is the world's most serious disease; so far, no complete cure has been discovered.

In 1900 the U.S. population was about 76 million; in 1998 the population was estimated at 269 million. The population of the world in 1900 was 1.6 billion; at the end of the twentieth century it is nearly three and a half times as large. The population of China alone is now 1.2 billion. In 1900 London was the world's most populous city, and the British ruled the world, occupying almost 20 percent of the globe and overseeing the lives of 25 percent of the world's population. Today Tokyo is the world's most populous city, the British Empire covers less than 1 percent of the earth's surface, and the United States is the world's most powerful nation.

Back in 1900, there were only forty-five states in the Union. Arizona, New Mexico, and Oklahoma were only territories, and Hawaii and Alaska were distant provinces. The American West was still pretty wild, and shoot-outs like those you've seen on TV still occurred.

More than 40 percent of American workers were farmers in 1900. In fact, so many children were needed to help with farm work that summer vacations from school became a policy—one you still benefit from. Today less than 3 percent of the workforce are farmers, and few American teenagers know the rigors of farm life.

If you were poor or an immigrant at the turn of the century, before child labor laws, you and your brothers and sisters as young as three years old would likely be picking cotton or fruit, digging sugar beets, or harvesting vegetables. In canneries, young kids husked corn, cut beans, peeled shrimp, and shucked oysters. In cities, children as young as ten worked twelve hours a day, six days a week, as glassblowers' assistants or at huge spinning machines in textile mills. At home, some children worked with their parents, making jewelry or artificial flowers. And in Pennsylvania, West Virginia, and other coal-producing states, nine- and ten-year-old boys worked as "breaker boys," separating coal from chunks of stone at the surface, while fourteen- and fifteen-year-olds worked long hours in the pitch dark and dangerous shafts of the mines. Education was not an option for those children and teenagers.

In fact, less than 5 percent of eighteen- to twenty-one-year-olds went to college back in 1900; nearly nine times that many do so now. And in some suburban communities, nearly every high-school graduate goes on to some form of higher education. In 1900, only 19 percent of college students were female; now, women make up more than 55 percent of the college population.

Back in 1900, only one out of every thirteen homes had a telephone. Only one in every seven homes had a bathtub! A dozen eggs cost 14 cents; a pound of butter cost 24 cents (in 1998 those items cost an average of $1.12 and $2.35, respectively). The good old American hamburger had just been invented, as had milk chocolate candy bars and Jell-O, but nobody had tasted Oreo cookies or Twinkies yet.

Although radio and television did not exist back then, that would soon change—and the world along with it. At the end of the twentieth century just about everyone owns several radios; the average American home contains two television sets, with three or four or more in some homes; 81 percent of American homes have a VCR. In 1900 a show could be seen only by the individuals who attended it; today that same event can be watched in millions of homes simultaneously, while being taped for future audiences.

As of 1998, 20 percent of American homes were connected to the Internet, with that number growing rapidly. Along with cellular phones and satellites, the Internet has made it possible for a person to communicate instantly with almost anyone anywhere, and the World Wide Web had made enormous amounts of information available at the touch of a computer key.

At the beginning of the twentieth century the Spanish-American War had just ended (in 1898), and the United States had become the most powerful nation in the world. There was then relative peace in the world, and people expected that to last a long time. But the Great War in

Europe soon changed that. When that terrible conflict ended, many people believed it had been the war that would end all wars. Unfortunately, the wars and assassinations of political leaders that characterized the early part of this century continued throughout the decades and persist to this day, with no end in sight. In 1998, for example, armed conflicts seethed in two dozen countries around the world, from Kosovo to the Congo, Sri Lanka to the Sudan.

Racial discrimination, too, seems never to end. People around the world are still being killed, mistreated, or excluded because of their ethnicity, their religion, or the color of their skin. The hate continues between Hutu and Tutsi people in Rwanda, for example, as does the animosity between Muslims and Christians in what used to be Yugoslavia, and between Arabs and Jews in the Middle East. Here in the United States, white supremacists still burn African American churches and sometimes murder black individuals. While the quality of life worldwide is much better at the end of the century, hate and violence persist.

The general health of the planet has also deteriorated. The elimination of rain forests around the world, especially in the Amazon basin, is now having global consequences. The survival of fewer trees, along with an increase in air pollution from greater industrialization, seems to be causing shrinkage of the ozone layer surrounding the planet, which provides some protection from the sun's ultraviolet rays. One thing is certain: Five of the warmest years of this century have occurred in the 1990s, with 1998 setting a new high for average worldwide temperature. Global warming has become one of the world's most serious threats.

Growing up at any time during the twentieth century, a typical teenager might have thought that all the interesting things in life had already occurred, and that the world was as modern as it possibly could be. Yet every decade has brought new changes—some frightening, some delightful, but all interesting. There's no doubt that more changes will occur in ways we can't even imagine now. At the same time, many things will remain the same, no matter who you are or where you live: the need for love and security; the fear of failure and of not being accepted; the joy of physical and mental accomplishments; the effort to be successful, to fight discrimination, to be somebody.

Here are ten stories about the lives of teenagers throughout the twentieth century, one story for each decade, that illustrate the continuing struggles of teenagers to understand themselves and make sense of their world.

So, if you're ready, let's open our time capsule and see what the twentieth century has been like for people your age.

1900 - 1909

The twentieth century began in peace and prosperity in America, and millions of people from Europe left poverty and persecution with the hope of a better life in the United States. The Wright brothers' first flight in an airplane and Henry Ford's first Model T automobiles promised marvelous things to come in transportation. The first radio broadcasts took place; the first double-sided records were produced; and the world's first moving (but silent) pictures were shown during this first decade. In sports, the first baseball World Series and the first international soccer game were held, and Americans went crazy for Ping-Pong. As they munched on new Hershey milk chocolate candy bars or chewed Barnum's Animal Crackers, kids were introduced to teddy bears and were able to draw with the world's first Crayola crayons in eight colors: red, yellow, blue, green, orange, violet, brown, and black.

To celebrate these good times and commemorate the

centennial of the Louisiana Purchase, the United States sponsored a World's Fair in St. Louis, Missouri, during the summer of 1904. In addition to displays from exotic cultures and exhibits of technological advances, visitors to the fair could sample hamburgers, frankfurters, iced tea, and ice cream in cones for the first time. Richard Peck, who wasn't born until 1934, heard stories about the fair from his aunt Geneva, who attended it as a girl of fourteen. Her descriptions of the fair "inflamed my childhood," Peck says. In "Electric Summer," he takes us back to the excitement and promise of the St. Louis World's Fair through the eyes of an Illinois farm girl.

The Electric Summer

by Richard Peck

I was sitting out there on the old swing that used to hang on the back porch. We'd fed Dad and the boys. Now Mama and I were spelling each other to stir the preserves. The screen door behind me was black with flies, and that smell of sugared strawberries cooking down filled all out-of-doors. A Maytime smell, promising summer.

Just turned fourteen, I was long-legged enough to push off the swing, then listen to the squeak of the chains. The swing was where I did my daytime dreaming. I sat there looking down past Mama's garden and the wind pump to the level line of long distance.

Like watching had made it happen, dust rose on the road from town. A black dot got bigger, scaring the sheep away from the fence line. It was an automobile. Nothing else churned the dust like that. Then by and by it was the Schumates' Oldsmobile, turning off the crown of the road and bouncing into our barn lot. There were only four automobiles in the town at that time, and only one of them driven by a woman—my aunt Elvera Schumate. She cut the motor off, but the Oldsmobile was still heaving. Climbing down, she put a gloved hand on a fender to calm it.

As Dad often said, Aunt Elvera would have been a novelty even without the automobile. In the heat of the day she wore a wide-brimmed canvas hat secured with a motoring veil tied under her chin. Her duster was a voluminous poplin garment, leather-bound at the hem.

My cousin Dorothy climbed down from the Olds, dressed similarly. They made a business of untangling themselves from their veils, propping their goggles up on their foreheads, and dusting themselves down the best they could. Aunt Elvera made for the house with Dorothy following. Dorothy always held back.

Behind me Mama banged on the screen door to scare the flies, then stepped outside. She was ready for a breather even if it meant Aunt Elvera. I stood up from the swing as Aunt Elvera came through the gate to the yard, Dorothy trailing. Where their goggles had been were two circles of clean skin around their eyes. They looked like a pair of raccoons. Mama's mouth twitched in something of a smile.

"Well, Mary." Aunt Elvera heaved herself up the porch steps and drew off her gauntlet gloves. "I can see you are having a busy day." Mama's hands were fire red from strawberry juice and the heat of the stove. Mine were scratched all over from picking every ripe berry in the patch.

"One day's like another on the farm," Mama remarked.

"Then I will not mince words," Aunt Elvera said, overlooking me. "I'd have rung you up if you were connected to the telephone system."

"What about, Elvera?" She and Mama weren't sisters. They were sisters-in-law.

"Why, the Fair, of course!" Aunt Elvera bristled in an important way. "What else? The Louisiana Purchase Exposition in St. Louis. The world will be there. It puts St. Louis at the hub of the universe." Aunt Elvera's mouth worked wordlessly.

"Well, I do know about it," Mama said. "I take it you'll be going?"

Aunt Elvera waved her away. "My stars, yes. You know how Schumate can be. Tight as a new boot. But I put my foot down. Mary, this is the opportunity of a lifetime. We will not see such wonders again during our span."

"Ah," Mama said, and my mind wandered—took a giant leap and landed in St. Louis. We knew about the Fair. The calendar the peddler gave us at Christmas featured a different pictorial view of the Fair for every month. There were white palaces in gardens with gondolas in waterways, everything electric-lit. Castles from Europe and paper houses from Japan. For the month of May the calendar featured the great floral clock on the fairgrounds.

"Send us a postal," Mama said.

"The thing is . . ." Aunt Elvera's eyes slid toward Dorothy. "We thought we'd invite Geneva to go with us."

My heart liked to lurch out of my apron. Me? They wanted to take me to the Fair?

"She'll be company for Dorothy."

Then I saw how it was. Dorothy was dim, but she could set her heels like a mule. She wanted somebody with her at the Fair so she wouldn't have to trail after her mother every minute. We were about the same age. We were in the same grade, but she was a year older, having repeated fourth grade. She could read, but her lips moved. And we were cousins, not friends.

"It will be educational for them both," Aunt Elvera said. "All the progress of civilization as we know it will be on display. They say a visit to the Fair is tantamount to a year of high school."

"Mercy," Mama said.

"We will take the Wabash Railroad directly to the gates of the Exposition," Aunt Elvera explained, "and we will be staying on the grounds themselves at the Inside Inn." She leaned nearer Mama, and her voice fell. "I'm sorry to say that there will be stimulants for sale on the fairgrounds. You know how St. Louis is in the hands of the breweries." Aunt Elvera was sergeant-at-arms of the Women's Christian Temperance Union, and to her, strong drink was a mocker. "But we will keep the girls away from that sort of thing." Her voice fell to a whisper. "And we naturally won't set foot on the Pike."

We knew what the Pike was. It was the midway of the Fair, like a giant carnival with all sorts of goings-on.

"Well, many thanks, but I don't think so," Mama said.

My heart didn't exactly sink. It never dawned on me that I'd see the Fair. I was only a little cast down because I might never get another glimpse of the world.

"Now, you're not to think of the money," Aunt Elvera said. "Dismiss that from your mind. Schumate and I will be glad to cover all Geneva's expenses. She can sleep in the bed with Dorothy, and we are carrying a good deal of our eats. I know these aren't flush times for farmers, Mary, but do not let your pride stand in Geneva's way."

"Oh, no," Mama said mildly. "Pride cometh before a fall. But we may be running down to the Fair ourselves."

Aunt Elvera's eyes narrowed, and I didn't believe Mama, either. It was just her way of fending off my aunt. Kept me from being in the same bed with Dorothy, too.

Aunt Elvera never liked taking no for an answer, but in time she and Dorothy made a disorderly retreat. We saw them off from the porch. Aunt Elvera had to crank the Olds to get it going while Dorothy sat up on the seat, adjusting the magneto or whatever it was. We watched Aunt Elvera's rear elevation as she stooped to jerk the crank time after time. If the crank got away from you, it could break your arm, and we watched to see if it would.

But at length the Olds coughed and sputtered to life. Aunt Elvera climbed aboard and circled the barn lot—she never had found the reverse gear. Then they were off back to town in a cloud of dust on the crown of the road.

I didn't want to mention the Fair, so I said, "Mama, would you ride in one of them things?"

"Not with Elvera running it," she said, and went back in the house.

I could tell you very little about the rest of that day. My mind was miles off. I know Mama wrung the neck off a fryer, and we had baking-powder biscuits to go with the warm jam. After supper my brothers hitched up Fanny to the trap and went into town. I took a bottle brush to the lamp chimneys and trimmed the wicks. After that I was back out on the porch swing while there was some daylight left. The lightning bugs were coming out, so that reminded me of how the Fair was lit up at night with electricity, brighter than day.

Then Mama came out and settled in the swing beside me, which was unusual, since she never sat out until the nights got hotter than this. We swung together awhile. Then she said in a quiet voice, "I meant it. I want you to see the Fair."

Everything stopped then. I still didn't believe it, but my heart turned over.

"I spoke to your dad about it. He can't get away, and he can't spare the boys. But I want us to go to the Fair."

Oh, she was brave to say it, she who hadn't been anywhere in her life. Brave even to think it. "I've got some egg money put back," she said. We didn't keep enough chickens to sell the eggs, but anything you managed to save was called egg money.

"That's for a rainy day," I said, being practical.

"I know it," she said. "But I'd like to see that floral clock."

Mama was famous for her garden flowers. When her glads were up, every color, people drove by to see them. And there was nobody to touch her for zinnias.

Oh, Mama, I thought, *is this just a game we're playing?* "What'll we wear?" I asked, to test her.

"They'll be dressy down at the Fair, won't they?" she said. "You know those artificial cornflowers I've got. I thought I'd trim my hat with them. And you're getting to be a big girl. Time you had a corset."

So then I knew she meant business.

*   *   *

That's how Mama and I went to the Louisiana Purchase Exposition in St. Louis that summer of 1904. We studied up on it, and Dad read the Fair literature along with us. Hayseeds we might be, but we meant to be informed hayseeds. They said the Fair covered twelve hundred acres, and we tried to see that in our minds, how many farms that would amount to. And all we learned about the Fair filled my heart to overflowing and struck me dumb with dread.

Mama weakened some. She found out when the Schumates were going, and we planned to go at the same time, just so we'd know somebody there. But we didn't take the same train.

When the great day came, Dad drove us to town, where the Wabash Cannonball stopped on its way to St. Louis. If he'd turned the trap around and taken us back home, you wouldn't have heard a peep out of me. And I think Mama was the same. But then we were on the platform with the big locomotive thundering in, everything too quick now, and too loud.

We had to scramble for seats in the day coach, lugging one straw valise between us and a gallon jug of lemonade. And a vacuum flask of the kind the Spanish-American War soldiers carried, with our own well water for brushing our teeth. We'd heard that St. Louis water came straight out of the Mississippi River, and there's enough silt in it to settle at the bottom of the glass. We'd go to their fair, but we weren't going to drink their water.

When the people sitting across from us went to the dining car, Mama and I spread checkered napkins over our knees and had our noon meal out of the valise. All the while, hot wind blew clinkers and soot in the window as we raced along like a crazed horse. Then a lady flounced up and perched on the seat opposite. She had a full bird on the wing sewed to the crown of her hat, and she was painted up like a circus pony, so we took her to be from Chicago. Leaning forward, she spoke, though we didn't know her from Adam. "Would you know where the ladies' rest room is?" she inquired.

We stared blankly back, but then Mama said politely, "No, but you're welcome to rest here till them other people come back."

The woman blinked at us, then darted away, hurrying now. I chewed on that a minute, along with my ham sandwich. Then I said, "Mama, do you suppose they have a privy on the train?"

"A *what*?" she said.

Finally, we had to know. Putting the valise on my seat and the hamper on hers, Mama and I went to explore. We walked through the swaying cars, from seat to seat, the cornflowers on Mama's hat aquiver. Sure enough, we came to a door at the end of a car with a sign reading LADIES. We crowded inside, and there it was. A water closet like you'd find in town and a chain hanging down and a roll of paper. "Well, I've seen everything now," Mama said. "You wouldn't catch me sitting on that thing in a moving train. I'd fall off."

But I wanted to know how it worked and reached for the handle on the chain. "Just give it a little jerk," Mama said.

We stared down as I did. The bottom of the pan was on a hinge. It dropped open, and there below were the ties of the Wabash tracks racing along beneath us.

We both jumped back and hit the door. And we made haste back to our seats. I guess we were lucky not to have found the lady with the bird on her hat in there, sitting down.

Then before I was ready, we were crossing the Mississippi River on a high trestle. There was nothing between us and the brown water. I put my hand over my eyes, but not before I glimpsed St. Louis on the far bank, sweeping away in the haze of heat as far as the eye could see.

We didn't stay at the Inside Inn. They wanted two dollars a night for a room, three if they fed you. We booked into a rooming house not far from the main gate, where we got a big square room upstairs with two beds for a dollar. It was run by a severe lady, Mrs. Wolfe, with a small, moon-faced son named Thomas clinging to her skirts. The place suited Mama, once she'd pulled down the bedclothes to check for bugs. It didn't matter where we laid our heads as long as it was clean.

We walked to the Fair that afternoon, following the crowds, trying to act like everybody else. Once again I'd have turned back if Mama had said to. It wasn't the awful grandeur of the pavilions rising white in the sun. It was all those people. I didn't know there were that many people in the world. They scared me at first, but then I couldn't see enough. My eyes began to drink deep.

We took the Intramural electric railroad that ran around the Exposition grounds, making stops. The Fair passed before us, and it didn't take me long to see what I was looking for. It was hard to miss. At the Palace of Transportation stop, I told Mama this was where we got off.

There it rose before us, 250 feet high. It was the giant wheel, the invention of George Washington Gale Ferris. A great wheel with thirty-six cars on it, each holding sixty people. It turned as we watched, and people were getting on and off like it was nothing to them.

"No power on earth would get me up in that thing," Mama murmured.

But I opened my hand and showed her the extra dollar Dad had slipped me to ride the wheel. "Dad said it would give us a good view of the Fair," I said in a wobbly voice.

"It would give me a stroke," Mama said. But then she set her jaw. "Your dad is putting me to the test. He thinks I won't do it."

Gathering her skirts, she moved deliberately toward the line of people waiting to ride the wheel.

We wouldn't look up while we waited, but we heard the creaking of all that naked steel. "That is the sound of doom," Mama muttered. Then, too soon, they were ushering us into a car, and I began to babble out of sheer fear.

"A lady named Mrs. Nicholson rode standing on the roof of one of these cars when the wheel was up at the Chicago fair, eleven years ago."

Mama turned to me. "What in the world for?"

"She was a daredevil, I guess."

"She was out of her mind," Mama said.

Now we were inside, and people mobbed the windows as we swooped up. I meant to stand in the middle of our car and watch the floor, but I looked out. In a moment we were above the roofs and towers of the Fair, a white city unfolding. There was the Grand Basin with the gondolas drifting. There was the mighty Festival Hall. Mama chanced a look.

It was cooler up there. My unforgiving Warner's Rust-Proof Corset had held me in a death grip all day, but I could breathe easier that high. Then we paused, dangling at the top. Now we were one with the birds, like hawks hovering over the Fair.

"How many wind pumps high are we?" Mama pondered. As we began to arch down again, we were both at a window, skinning our eyes to see the Jerusalem exhibit and the Philippine Village and, way off, the Plateau of States—a world of wonders.

Giddy when we got out, we staggered on solid ground and had to sit down on an ornamental bench. Now Mama was game for anything. "If they didn't want an arm and a leg for the fare," she said, "I'd ride that thing again. Keep the ticket stubs to show your dad we did it."

Braver than before, we walked down the Pike, as it was still broad daylight. It was lined with sidewalk cafes in front of all manner of attractions: the Streets of Cairo and the Palais du Costume, Hagenbeck's Circus and a replica of the Galveston flood. Because we were parched, we found a table at a place where they served a new drink, tea with ice in it. "How do we know we're not drinking silt?" Mama wondered, but it cooled us off.

As quick as you'd sit down anywhere at the Fair, there'd be entertainment. In front of the French Village they had a supple young man named Will Rogers doing rope tricks. And music? Everywhere you turned, and all along the Pike, the song the world sang that summer was: "Meet me in St. Louis, Louis, meet me at the fair."

We sat over our tea and watched the passing parade. Some of those people you wouldn't want to meet in a dark alley. Over by the water chutes a gang of rough men waited to glimpse the ankles of women getting out of the boats. But the only thing we saw on the Pike we shouldn't have was Uncle Schumate weaving out of the saloon bar of the Tyrolean Alps.

I can't tell all we saw in our two days at the Fair. We tried to look at things the boys and Dad would want to hear about—the Hall of Mines and Metallurgy, and the livestock. We learned a good deal of history: the fourteen female statues to stand for the states of the Louisiana Purchase of 1803, and the log cabin that President U. S. Grant had been born in. But most of what we saw foretold the future: automobiles and airships and moving pictures.

Our last night was the Fourth of July. Fifty bands played, some of them on horseback. John Philip Sousa, in gold braid and white, conducted his own marches. Lit in every color, the fountains played to this music and the thunder of the fireworks. And the cavalry from the Boer War exhibit rode in formation, brandishing torches.

Mama turned away from all the army uniforms, thinking of my brothers, I suppose. But when the lights came on, every tower and minaret picked out with electric bulbs, we saw what this new century would be: all the grandeur of ancient Greece and Rome, lit by lightning. A new century, with the United States of America showing the way. But you'd have to run hard not to be left behind.

We saved the floral clock for our last morning. It lay across a hillside next to the Agriculture Palace, and it was beyond anything we'd ever seen. The dial of it was 112 feet across, and each giant hand weighed 2,500 pounds. It was all made of flowers, even the numbers. Each Hour Garden had plants that opened at that time of day, beginning with morning glories. We stood in a rapture, waiting for it to strike the hour.

Then who appeared before us with her folding Kodak camera slung around her neck but Aunt Elvera Schumate. To demonstrate her worldliness, she merely nodded like we were all just coming out of church back home. "Well, Mary," she said to Mama, "I guess this clock shames your garden."

Mama dipped her head modestly to show the corn-flowers on her hat. "Yes, Elvera," she said, "I am a humbler woman for this experience," and Aunt Elvera didn't quite know what to make of her reply. "Where's Dorothy?" Mama asked innocently.

"That child!" Aunt Elvera said. "I couldn't get her out of the bed at the Inside Inn! She complains of blistered feet. Wait till she has a woman's corns! I am a martyr to mine. I cannot get her interested in the Fair. She got as far as the bust of President Roosevelt sculpted in butter, but then she faded." Aunt Elvera cast me a baleful look, as if this was all my fault. "Dorothy is going through a phase."

But there Aunt Elvera was wrong. Dorothy never was much better than that for the rest of her life. Mama didn't inquire into Uncle Schumate's whereabouts; we thought we knew.

* * *

On the train ride home we were seasoned travelers, Mama
and I. When the candy butcher hawked his wares through
our car, we knew to turn our faces away from his prices. We
crossed the Mississippi River on that terrible trestle, and
after Edwardsville the land settled into flat fields. Looking
out, Mama said, "Corn's knee high by the Fourth of July,"
because she was thinking ahead to home. "I'll sleep good
tonight without those streetcars clanging outside the window."

But they still clanged in my mind, and "The Stars and
Stripes Forever" blended with "Meet Me in St. Louis,
Louis."

"But Mama, how can we just go home after all we've
seen?"

Thinking that over, she said, "You won't have to, you
and the boys. It's your century. It can take you wherever
you want to go." Then she reached over and put her hand
on mine, a thing she rarely did. "I'll keep you back if I can.
But I'll let you go if I must."

That thrilled me, and scared me. The great world
seemed to swing wide like the gates of the Fair, and I
didn't even have a plan. I hadn't even put up my hair yet.
It seemed to me it was time for that, time to jerk that big
bow off the braid hanging down my back and put up my
hair in a woman's way.

"Maybe in the fall," said Mama, who was turning into a
mind reader as we steamed through the July fields, heading for home.

Richard Peck

Winner of the Margaret A. Edwards Award for lifetime achievement, the ALAN Award for his contributions to young adult literature, and the Empire State Award from the New York Library Association, Richard Peck is the author of two dozen novels for young adults that are filled with wry humor as well as thought-provoking insights into teenage life. Nearly half of his novels have been designated Best Books for Young Adults by the American Library Association, with *Are You in the House Alone?* being voted one of the 100 Best of the Best Books for Young Adults published between 1967 and 1992. That novel also won the Edgar Allan Poe Juvenile Mystery Award in 1977.

Some of his novels, such as *The Dreadful Future of Blossom Culp*, *Secrets of the Shopping Mall*, and *Bel-Air Bambi and the Mall Rats*, are more funny than serious. Others, such as *Are You in the House Alone?*, *Remembering the Good Times*, *The Last Safe Place on Earth*, and his recent *Strays Like Us*, explore serious problems experienced by contemporary teenagers, such as rape, suicide, abandonment, peer pressure, a parent with AIDS, and censorship.

Time travel is featured in three of Peck's Blossom Culp novels and in *Voices After Midnight*, as well as in his more recent *Lost in Cyberspace* and its sequel, *The Great Interactive Dream Machine*. In *Lost in Cyberspace*, two sixth-grade boys in a New York City private school use a computer to travel back in time; in the sequel, Aaron discovers that his computer can grant wishes, with hilarious consequences. *The*

Great American Dream Machine appears on *Voice of Youth Advocates'* list of the Best Science Fiction, Fantasy, and Horror of 1996.

Peck has also published four novels for adults, several essays for teachers and librarians, a variety of poems, and a number of short stories, including the now-famous "Priscilla and the Wimps." His most recent book, in fact, is a collection of connected short stories that follow the experiences of a teenage boy and his younger sister who visit their resourceful grandmother in a small Illinois town each summer between 1929 and 1935. If you enjoy adventurous tall tales with larger-than-life characters, you'll want to read *A Long Way from Chicago*. It was a National Book Award finalist in 1998 and a 1999 Newbery Honor Book.

Peck has always been nostalgic for the early years of the twentieth century, a fact that shows itself in several of his novels, including the Blossom Culp series and his time-travel books, as well as in the story you just read. He even has a memento from the 1904 St. Louis World's Fair catching the light on the windowsill of his New York City apartment: a ruby cup etched with his father's name that his aunt Geneva brought back for her younger brother.

You can find out more about Richard Peck in his autobiography, *Anonymously Yours*.

1910 - 1919

When Halley's Comet shot across the sky at the start of the second decade, some people saw it as an omen of terrible future events. And their fears came true. The "unsinkable" *Titanic* sank during its first Atlantic crossing; war broke out across Europe, causing the deaths of nearly ten million people; the Russian people revolted against Czar Nicholas II and Communist rule was established in the Soviet Union; and in 1918, an epidemic of Spanish flu killed more than twenty million people around the world.

At the same time, industrial and scientific progress made electric food mixers and pop-up toasters available to homemakers. The Panama Canal was opened, and the National Park System was established. The first brand-name sneakers were sold; the zipper was invented; and the first liquid nail polish was created. Aunt Jemima pancake flour was introduced, as was Franco-American canned spaghetti, and kids across the country had their first taste of Oreo cookies and Life Savers candy.

While that was going on, many American workers were trading their farm jobs for factory work. This was especially true of black families who left the rural South in search of higher wages and better treatment in northern cities.

But it was the Great War in Europe that changed society the most. Once the United States entered the fray, the entire country was mobilized to deal with it. The government took over railroads, coal mines, telephones, and food distribution, suspending individual liberties and legislating patriotism. Against this backdrop, Jeanette Ingold introduces us to an observant Texas teenager in 1918 who steps onto a streetcar and faces a world she has to struggle to understand.

Moving On

by Jeanette Ingold

It's strange, how something ordinary as a screen door opening can be the sound of a person's world jumping its tracks.

That's what I'm hearing, though, when Thel lets herself in the back. "Mornin', Tashie," she says, and goes on to the dining room, where my mother is putting away crystal.

"Ma'am," I hear Thel say, "I need to tell you today will be my last." She says it just like that: Thel, our colored girl who's been in and out of this house all my life.

Mama says, "Your last! Whatever do you mean?"

Leaving my breakfast, I push through the swinging door as Thel answers, "I'll be moving on."

"But you belong here," I burst out.

Thel's eyes flick my way.

We were playmates when her mother did washing and cleaning here and would bring Thel along. And since Thel turned sixteen two years ago, old enough to take over, she's been the one coming in five and a half days a week.

How can she leave?

Thel offers nothing more, and Mama has to pry just to learn that Thel's husband, George, quit his job sweeping up at the railway depot. Now Thel and George and their baby are leaving Dallas and moving to Pittsburgh.

"I'll just get on with the hand laundry," Thel says, letting us know that she's done talking.

When I return to my late breakfast, the cereal is soggy and the pitcher of milk turned warm in a shaft of sunlight.

Once my world's bumped off course, it continues lurching along of its own accord through this Saturday of 1918.

First Mama calls, "Tashie, have you seen my filigree pin?"

"No," I answer, and go to help her hunt through gloves and handkerchiefs. "Maybe it's still pinned to a dress?"

It's not, however, and neither Thel nor my cousin Luce, who's visiting this summer, can suggest where it might be.

Mama is upset way more than misplacing a pin calls for, even if it is her favorite, and I have to think it's because of how she feels about Thel.

"Nobody is going anywhere until that pin is found," she says, and I see Luce roll her eyes. Luce and I have plans for a movie matinee, not for a day spent turning the house upside down.

Thank goodness Luce finally thinks to say, "Aunt Elizabeth, could you have left it at Grandmother's?"

"Well, perhaps I did," Mama answers.

Then Thel and I have words over her leaving and being so close-mouthed about why.

Lunch is done and Thel's washing dishes when I go into the kitchen to confront her myself. "You can't really want to go away from here, where you were raised and all your people are."

Thel takes a dish towel to the last cups without answering.

"I'd be afraid of going to the North," I say, "not knowing anybody, being squished elbow to elbow in some Yankee city with people who don't know who you are, or care."

Thel still doesn't look at me, but a sudden tremor in her hand makes the cup she's putting away click sharply against a hook.

And seeing she is scared makes me snap, "Well, I just don't understand."

"You just don't need to," she snaps back.

We glare at each other a long moment before Thel picks up the pan of rinse water and carries it outside to dump by Mama's roses.

Luce, who's come in the kitchen in time to hear the last part, says, "Tashie, I can't believe you let her talk to you that way."

I shrug. "She usually doesn't." Not in years, anyway, not since Thel and I were little kids racing through games together and Thel was as free to best me as I was her.

"My mother," Luce goes on, "says never permit them to sass."

I can see Thel at the clothesline, checking how the undergarments she washed are drying. "Luce," I tell my cousin, "hush up."

"Why?" Luce asks, surprised.

"Just hush."

Now the three of us are waiting for the streetcar, Luce flirting with a couple of soldiers and Thel and me standing
apart both from her and from each other.

Around us, though, this out-of-control world seems to
be picking up speed, everything and everybody else on
Bryan Street flying this way or that and the sun itself join-
ing in the motion.

It rises in heat waves off the pavement and glistens on
the sweaty backs of horses pulling an ice wagon. It ripples
in the polished fenders of a new Buick automobile and
sparkles from marbles my little brother is shooting out of a
chalked ring.

And surely a few blocks away that sun is bouncing off
the streetcar that will soon rush toward us, leashed to over-
head electric lines as if, turned loose, it might go who
knows where.

Go who knows where, same as Thel.

My cousin calls, "Thel, watch your foot," as a cat's-eye
spins her way.

The marble rolls against her tote bag, the one she uses
to take leftovers home to her family. I heard Mama tell her,
"You fill it good now," and gave her a precious bit of ham
and a loaf of victory bread made without white flour. It was
Mama's way of saying good-bye.

Thel bends down to send back the marble and then
straightens up without looking my way.

I make my gaze sweep past her, on to my cousin.

The soldiers Luce is flirting with are Barker Haines,

from around the corner, and a Yankee friend he's brought home from training camp. "Well, I never," she's saying, pretending disbelief at some tale of northern strangeness.

I have to smile at that, because nothing really shocks Luce. She's eighteen, two years older than me, and staying with my family while her parents are in Washington, D.C. Her father—my uncle on Papa's side—is doing dollar-a-year work, donating his time to a war administration job, and Aunt Sarah is something important with the Red Cross. And Luce . . .

Sophisticated. That's the word I want to describe Luce. Soft-spoken, pretty, and dripping elegance, and I'm hoping to catch some before this summer is out. She's promised I will and already is working on Mama to let me bob my hair, though I can't imagine Mama saying yes to something so daring.

I look away before the young men see me gawking, and once more my gaze passes over Thel, so quick I catch her studying me.

And then the streetcar slides in, bell clanging and wheels clacking on the rails. Barker and his friend take their leave, and I follow my cousin onto the trolley. We each drop seven cents into the fare box and take the bench behind the motorman.

A moment later, Thel pays her own way and walks past us to the back.

We're late getting to the picture show. The darkened theater is almost full, both the downstairs and the colored balcony, and the piano player is laughing along with everyone else at the antics of a Mack Sennett comedy.

"This must be about over," Luce whispers as we work our way toward two seats close to the front.

An official war review comes on next. It starts with pictures of the fighting in France, soldiers running from trenches to scramble over the barbed wire of no-man's-land. Then it switches to the ordered ranks of a company of Negro soldiers marching across a parade ground.

A caption says to remember the important work being done at home, and we see cavalry troops patrolling the Mexican border; a freighter being loaded by women stevedores; long lines of workmen, white and colored both, disappearing through the vast doors of a steel mill.

There's a pause while the projectionist changes film reels, and Luce says she thinks those female dockworkers must not have good sense. "Dressing like men," she says. "Getting filthy dirty. I can just imagine what their hands are like."

Luce stops talking long enough to examine her own hands. Even in the dimness her fingernails shine with Cutex's new liquid polish, which she's also trying to talk Mama into allowing me to use.

Finally the picture we've come to see—*Prunella*, featuring Marguerite Clark—begins. A few minutes into it, though, the film jumps and then abruptly stops.

"It'll be just a moment, folks," the projectionist calls.

"Wouldn't you know?" Luce says. "Tashie, tell me about Barker Haines. I think he's taken with me."

"Just from one visit at a streetcar stop?" I ask.

"Well, no," Luce answers. "I might have run into him once or twice earlier." She touches my wrist and leans closer. "Actually, just once before, but I was wearing that embroidered voile dress Mama sent me all the way from Washington, and your mama's sweet filigree pin at the neck, and—"

"Mama's pin?" I interrupt. "She lent it to you?"

"Of course not, not so she knew. I borrowed it like I do my own mother's things that she might think are too old for me."

"So Mama didn't leave it at Grandmother's?"

"No, I just told you, Tashie," Luce says. "Though to be honest, I'd forgotten I still had the pin, until it turned up missing this morning."

I think of all the time wasted searching. "But why didn't you just give it back?"

"Tashie, if I had," Luce says, sounding as though she's explaining the obvious to a child, "then your mother would have known I'd been poking into her bureau and doing things behind her back. I can't have Aunt Elizabeth thinking I'd be so ill-mannered."

"But—"

"Will you stop saying *but*? Before we left, I put the pin where she's sure to have found it by now."

The movie comes back on just then, but the picture is jumping even worse than before. Cutting it off again, the projectionist calls, "This time will be the charm, folks. I promise."

This time, though, the house lights get turned on, and immediately after that a man wearing a business suit vaults onto the stage. He tells the audience, "I bet you all didn't know there was a Four Minute Man planted among you, just in case four minutes popped up ready to be filled."

Waving down laughter and mock groans, he launches into a prepared speech about our valiant soldiers and how they need our nickels and dimes, our dollars and our work.

"So, Luce," I whisper, "exactly where did you leave Mama's pin?"

"In the wash basket," Luce answers, "between the chemises and some folded drawers."

"But . . ." I stare at her, aghast. "Luce, Mama is bound to think Thel put it there."

"Of course," Luce says. "She'll suppose Thel was going to steal the pin and then thought better of it."

"Luce," I begin, but I hardly know what to say to make my cousin see how wrong that is.

"Tashie," she tells me, "it's not like it matters. And Thel's never coming back, anyway."

On the stage, the Four Minute Man starts a chorus of "Over There," and I have to raise my voice for Luce to hear me over the singing.

"It does matter," I tell her. "Luce, either you've got to tell Mama or I will."

At that, my cousin's eyes narrow, all the prettiness disappearing. "You say one word," she warns me, "and I will just have to tell your mother how sorry I am to report the real truth. Aunt Elizabeth is going to be so sad to hear how *you* took her pin to wear on your party dress the other night. You do remember, don't you? How you climbed out a window and slipped away to the soldiers' canteen? Of course, I'll have to apologize for covering up for—"

"Luce," I break in, "you know none of that's true. Mama won't believe you."

"Maybe she will and maybe she won't," Luce answers. "But it will make her wonder. Little cousin, it will be a cold day on the equator before your mother again trusts you as surely as she used to."

I can feel myself shrink into the place Luce has made for me, while the audience beats out the rhythmic last syllables of "Over There."

"And until the fighting is done over there and we and our allies have defeated the German menace," says the Four Minute Man, "our soldiers need all our help defending liberty."

He points to a woman. "Madam," he says, "will you be the first to pledge purchase of a twenty-five-cent war Thrift Stamp right after today's picture show?"

He waits for her yes before turning his attention to a man a few rows back. "You, sir, are you giving all you can to the Liberty Loan?"

The man answers, "Twice that, just like the loan committee demanded," which gets a knowing laugh from the audience.

"And you, sir." The Four Minute Man addresses a shirt-sleeved fellow sitting two chairs down from me. "Are you giving your all for Lady Liberty?"

The poor guy, who's not more than thirty, blushes, and the Four Minute Man jokes, "I'm not asking about your sweetheart, young fellow. I'm asking what you're doing to preserve our country's freedom."

Still the fellow doesn't respond. I can see him clearly. His eyes shift this way and that, and he seems to burrow into his chair.

"Say," someone calls, "why aren't you in the service, anyway?" and another person mutters, "Ask if he's a Kraut-lover."

This isn't what the Four Minute Man wants, and he tries to help the guy out. "I bet you're doing necessary war work," he says, "defending liberty in your own way." He motions to the pianist to get things moving along, but before she can play a note, there's a holler of "Slacker," and from somewhere a spitball splotches wet against the young man's neck.

I see how he wipes it off and, as though disbelieving, examines the wetness on the palm of his hand. Another spitball hits him, and another, before he half stands, turning toward the audience, looking cornered. When he speaks, his voice is partly proud and partly muffled in surliness.

"I'll be a soldier when the draft board makes me," he says, "and not until. But I won't lend money to protect liberties that have already been taken away."

There's a growing buzz of whispers all over the main floor now, and someone yells, "Disloyalist."

"If you think I'm wrong," the man says, "then ask yourselves just what rights you've got left, now that this war's taken over everything. How about you shopkeepers? Are you deciding what you'll sell and how you'll price it, or is the government doing that for you?"

His voice grows louder as he tries to make himself heard over an angry growl. "You housewives, when was the last time you cooked a meal without worrying whether you were forgetting meatless Tuesday or porkless Thursday or God knows what Hooverism?"

An elderly woman says, "Don't take the Lord's name in vain, young man," but mostly there's just yelling in the theater now, angry words like *treason* and *sedition* being hurled. And then suddenly several men have the guy by the arms and are hustling him outside.

Someone says, "I hope they get the police after him."

"He deserves to be taught a lesson," Luce tells me. "It's against the law, talking out about our country's policies like that."

Up on the stage, the Four Minute Man struggles to regain control. "People, people, let's get back our good spirit," he says. "How about more music?"

The piano player picks "You're in the Army Now," and after a moment everybody is singing, as though glad to have funny words to turn their mind to.

Then, for a final time, the house lights go out, and the audience settles down to watching *Prunella*. Instead of the story on the screen, though, I keep seeing how that young man looked when he was being shoved up the aisle. His face was flushed, and he must have been scared, but his eyes weren't shifting about anymore. They were looking straight at his accusers. And he was bigger than he'd seemed when he was huddled in his seat.

He was wrong to say what he did about the government. . . . I'm sure he was, getting the facts right but mixing up what they all meant . . . but at least he stood up for what he believed. There must be something honorable in that.

Luce is all silly prattle as we wait our turn to board the streetcar home, carrying on as though she'd never made the threat she did. "Isn't Marguerite Clark just the dearest thing?" she says. "And how I would love to meet a man like . . ."

She steps onto the trolley, and I start to follow her and then suddenly know that I can't, any more than that young man in the theater could stay in his seat. "Tell Mama I'll be along in a bit," I tell Luce. Then I turn and cross to where there's another streetcar stop for people headed the other way.

I ignore Luce calling to me, "Tashie, where are you going?"

I get directions from the trolley conductor for where I need to transfer and how far I should stay on after that. Within blocks after changing, I'm in a part of town I've only ridden through with Papa when he's taken Thel home because it was late or she was carrying bundles of ironing.

Thel doesn't live right on the car line, but when I recognize the corner stores where she shops, I push the stop button to buzz the motorman.

"Are you sure this is where you want?" the conductor asks as I wait for the center door to open.

"Yes, thank you," I answer, sounding firm so he won't argue.

I go three or four blocks before I reach the dirt road Thel's house is on. This close to Saturday supper, there are lots of people out and about, visiting in the neighborhood, but I'm the only white person. No one says anything to me except for an occasional "Afternoon," or a man stepping aside and tipping his cap: "Miss."

Finally I reach Thel's place, which is an unpainted clapboard cottage with a covered porch, both ends of it settled lower than the middle. I'm about to knock on the door when her husband opens it. Without asking me in, George nods and says he'll get Thel.

And then she's standing in the open doorway, her baby hanging on her legs. "Yes?" she says, her eyes asking all the questions that the word doesn't.

And I realize I don't know what I want to say. "He's growing," I finally manage, pointing to her little boy.

On the wall behind Thel there's a photograph of a soldier, and after thinking a moment I realize it must be her brother. "Is that Joe?" I ask. "I thought he was doing farm work back in East Texas."

"He gone to Chicago when the cotton failed a couple years back."

"And then he got drafted?" I ask.

Thel nods, and after that there's an awkward silence, which she finally breaks by asking, "You gonna tell me why you come?"

"To say a better good-bye, I guess. And to wish you well, even if you won't tell me why you're going."

"And I wish you well," Thel says. She steps back as though expecting me to leave now, but when I don't, she asks, "There more?"

Yes.

"Thel," I blurt, "I just wanted to say . . . to tell you . . . I want you to know that I'll make sure people remember you right."

I can see that she's puzzled, and of course she has no way of knowing what I'm talking about, and I've no way to tell her without parading out family matters, which I can't do. "I just wanted you to hear it," I say.

My voice trails off as we stand there, what we know of each other lying between us, as well as all we don't.

"Well," I finally say, "I better go now, while the streetcar's still running."

"Get a transfer," Thel tells me, "so you don't pay two fares."

"I'll remember. Good-bye, Thel. I *do* wish you well." Then I turn and start away.

"Say," Thel calls after me, "what movie you see?"

"That new one with Marguerite Clark."

"You see that picture come first, men like George goin' in that factory?"

I nod.

"It's good wages," Thel says. "You asked why. That's part."

I wait a moment, giving her a chance to explain more, but Thel has said all she's going to, and I suppose I have, too.

She does go inside then, closing the door behind her, and I can imagine her returning to her packing, or fixing food for the journey. She's got a family to prepare for moving on.

And I've got a streetcar to catch, and Mama and Luce to face, and then I guess I'll move on from wherever that takes me.

Jeanette Ingold

Streetcars that hinted of an earlier era still ran along Bryan Street when Jeanette Ingold visited Dallas as a youngster. "Every trolley ride offered some thrill of adventure," she recalls. Remembering those experiences gave her the beginning for the story "Moving On." But since writers like to write about the things they wish to explore, Ingold set her story in the period between 1910 and 1920, which she found "an exciting place for viewing both what was and what would be coming." In 1918, at the end of World War I, people, events, and technologies were moving at a breathtaking pace, prompting people to examine who they were, where they were going, and how they fit in.

A former teacher and newspaper reporter, Jeanette Ingold likes to write about teenagers who want to know more about themselves and the inventions of their times, are curious about where they come from, and are ready to move into a brighter future. Her first novel for young people, *The Window,* is narrated by fifteen-year-old Mandy, who has been blinded in a car accident that killed her mother. Sent to live on a Texas farm with elderly relatives she has never met, Mandy struggles to accustom herself to these quiet and loving people while dealing with her blindness among strangers in the local high school. Before long, through the window of her upstairs bedroom, she hears voices and "sees" events from years earlier that slowly reveal her family's mysterious history. *The Window* was named a Best Book for Young Adults by the American Library Association in 1997, as well as a 1998 International

Reading Association Young Adults' Choices book, and was also nominated for the Missouri Mark Twain Award and the Indiana Young Hoosier Award.

In *Pictures, 1918,* against the background of World War I and anti-German feeling, fifteen-year-old Asia explores her relationships with her parents, aging grandmother, neighbor Nick, and Nick's cousin Boy. Longing to own a special Autographic camera she sees in the window of the local drugstore, Asia first apprentices herself to a supportive photographer in her small Texas town and then begins to capture images of her community and loved ones. Along the way, she comes to understand the people around her and to recognize her own potential. This novel was nominated in 1998 for the ALA Best Books for Young Adults and ALA Quick Picks lists and was a New York Public Library Book for the Teen Age.

Ingold's latest book, *Airfield,* follows the exploits of two teenagers who find jobs at a small-town airport in 1933 when air travel is still for the adventurous and the fledgling airline industry offers a promising future to young people.

Jeanette Ingold was born and raised in New York, but she finds many of her stories in her family's home state of Texas. She now lives with her husband on the outskirts of Missoula, Montana, where she likes to take photographs, garden, and travel back roads when she isn't writing.

You can learn more about Jeanette Ingold on her Web site at www.jeanetteingold.com.

After the Great War, life in America changed radically in many ways. Electricity was brought to most areas of the country; radio programs expanded; and television was invented, though there was little to watch. Railroads and a national highway system were developed; Charles Lindbergh thrilled the world with the first nonstop solo flight across the Atlantic Ocean; and Germany's *Graf Zeppelin* completed a circumnavigation of the world in twenty-one days.

As African Americans became more prosperous, black writers and artists flourished. Unfortunately, white racism in the form of the Ku Klux Klan also increased. Women, too, attained more personal freedom during the twenties, tried more daring clothing and lifestyles, and gained the right to vote with the passing of the Nineteenth Amendment.

During the decade, the National Football League was formed, as was the National Negro Baseball League. The first Winter Olympics was held. And Babe Ruth signed with the New York Yankees, hitting fifty-four home runs his first year and sixty in 1927. Penicillin was discovered, the first frozen foods were introduced, the first issues of *Reader's Digest* and *Time* were published, and Fleer's Dubble Bubble gum was invented.

But the most dominant impression of the decade has always been captured in the words *the Roaring Twenties*. People entertained themselves with movies, dancing, and jazz. Instead of putting a damper on partying, the passing of the Eighteenth Amendment to the Constitution in 1920, prohibiting the transportation and sale of alcoholic beverages, made nightclubs and "speakeasy" bars with their "bootleg" liquor even more attractive. But it was not all fun for everybody, as you will see in the following story about a Minnesota farm boy who is drawn into the world of bootlegging, gangsters, and corruption.

1920-1929

Bootleg Summer

by Will Weaver

We have become a gangsters' mecca, and the rules
are simple: check in on arrival, pay off the officials,
and commit no crimes within the city limits. Some
gangsters are reputed to have bought lake homes in
northern Wisconsin and Minnesota to be closer to
the Canadian border. Life in the north allows gangsters to escape the heat—in more ways than one!
—*Minneapolis Tribune editorial, "The Saint Paul
Layover" (1925)*

Dead dragonflies and grasshoppers litter the road. Them
and a run-over garter snake split open and dried like a strip
of jerky. But I don't deserve better company: I am the low-
est thing that ever lived.

Oh, sure, I look normal. Drive up behind me and you'll
see a young fella with yellow hair thick as a shock of
Minnesota wheat and a knapsack over his shoulder. I'm
wearing dungarees and boots, and I'm passably clean—I
don't look criminal. But don't stop to give me a ride. Pass

me by in a cloud of dust, swear at me, pitch a rotten to-
mato at me—I don't care. What I done this summer, I
wouldn't even stop to give myself a ride.

But sure enough, a horn toots and a big Packard slows
alongside. It's a free country; I can't stop the fool from
offering me a seat up front.

"How far you going, son?" the driver asks.

"Minneapolis, St. Paul, it don't matter," I mutter.

"The Twin Cities! That's a mighty long way."

"The farther away the better," I answer bitterly.

"Had enough of the farm, then?" He chuckles as he
swings open the door.

I take a closer look at him as I get in. He's a middle-
aged man with a cheap fedora that's shiny around the
brim—he's probably a drummer of some kind, which is
another word for traveling salesman. Or he could be a tin-
ker looking to repair pots and pans. He's got two trunks in
the backseat, but I can't tell what's in 'em. Anyway, dime a
dozen, his type. Every month some salesman like him came
to our farm selling Watkins' products, or salves and lotions,
or "miracle cures" of some kind. But I never seen a salesman drive a car this nice.

"Every week I see farm boys on the road," he says as he
motors us back onto the pavement, "and I always give them
a ride 'cause I grew up on a farm myself. Let me tell you,
there's easier ways to make a buck than shoveling cow
dung." He shakes tobacco out of his Bull Durham pouch
and begins rolling a cigarette with one hand (a guy driving
a car this nice ought to be smoking a big stogie, I think).
"Me, I couldn't wait to get to the big city where they had

electric lights and movies," he continues. "Heck, now they got movies that talk and girls that dance the Lindy hop and speakeasies on every corner."

"I don't much care about that stuff," I mutter.

He gives me a sideways glance. "Then what you leaving home for?"

I don't answer him. I can't talk about it 'cause the words bunch up in my throat like a hairball. I might even bawl like a baby.

"Quiet type, eh? Well, suit yourself," the salesman says. He starts talking about all the driving he does; about all the strange ducks he has given rides to; about all the interesting accidents he's seen. This goes on for nearly a half hour—until I can't stand it anymore.

"I left home 'cause I killed two men," I blurt out.

The Packard swerves and his cigarette pitches out the window, and suddenly he's got a crowbar in his hand. "Don't you try anything with me, kid!"

"Don't worry, I didn't kill them with my own hands," I say, looking off across the fields. "But I might as well have."

The car slows but keeps rolling. "Kid, you ain't on the lam or anything, are you? I don't need no problems with the law." His eyes flicker to the backseat.

"I ain't on the lam," I say. *Except maybe from my own self,* I think.

"Well, if you want to keep riding with me, you better spill the beans."

I realize that's what I been wanting to do ever since things came to a head, which was four days ago.

"You ain't fully wrong about the farm," I begin. "My

father raised hogs, and to me they never stunk until this year. That's probably because everybody I knew always smelled like some kind of livestock, especially in grade school. But last year I had to start high school in town—I'm sixteen, if you want to know—and on my first day of school, Melinda Anderson—she's the banker's daughter—wrinkled up her nose at me and called out, 'Soooooowee! I smell hogs!' "

The drummer clucks his tongue in sympathy.

"Everybody laughed," I continue. "When I got home that afternoon it was like my nose came unstuffed for the first time in my life. I couldn't stand the smell of hogs after that, which was a problem, because hogs pay the bills on our farm."

"But you still up and left," he says, rolling a fresh cigarette.

"No sir, not right away. I wouldn't do that to my daddy. He ain't the worst father in the world. I did a little sniffing around town, then I talked to my mother. I told her that the PureOil Station on Main Street was looking for a part-time man to fix tires and do mechanic work. I told her that if I got the job, I could pay for a farm hand—someone to replace me—from my wages. What I didn't tell her was I'd already landed the job and was supposed to start soon as I could."

"Plenty of work around nowadays," the salesman says with a nod. "Never seen things so good as they are this year. But what'd your old man have to say about things?"

"He was for me working off the farm like frost in July, like teats on a boar. But my mother, she's a reader and she's good with words. She told him that there was more to the world for young men than slopping hogs and breaking land. And for that matter, there was more to the world for women than butchering chickens and canning corn and carrying water and darning socks by lantern light. She said that in town at least people had power and light. Houses had a lightbulb in every room; people had clothes washers with motor-driven paddles and power wringers—they even had electric iceboxes and radios. She said compared to that, the kerosene lamp in our living room cast a mighty small circle of light."

The salesman is silent for a spell. "What'd she mean by that?"

"I ain't sure, but it made my father stop and think, too." I pause. "Gosh, I'll miss them," I blurt out.

"Sure, kid, sure," he says. "But who was it that got killed?"

For some reason I don't want to rush my story. I want to tell everything exactly how it happened.

"Anyway, I went to work at the PureOil Station that same week," I continue. "They gave me a shirt with my name on it, and after a month, I got my own PureOil cap, white with blue pinstripes." I was so proud of that uniform—prouder than of anything I'd ever owned.

The drummer flicks his cigarette ash impatiently. Funny how I want to go on about that uniform.

"Anyway, the owner, Mr. Stevens, he was an all-right man. And the manager, Bob, he was mostly okay, though he made me stay in the back room and do the dirty work while he ran the gas pumps and talked to people."

"Go on," the drummer says.

"Except for this one day when I heard a horn toot, and suddenly Bob comes rushing into the back room all pasty-faced, like he's seen a ghost. He says to me, 'Kid—catch the drive! There's a man out there wants gas and you'd damn well better give it to him.'

"So I jump up real quick and head out to the drive. And what a car for my first time! Big chrome headlamps, the hood as long as a boat deck, the upright windshield and the square, gray roof and the window curtains in back—I'd never seen a real car like it, but I knew what it was right away: a 1927 Pierce-Arrow four-passenger coach."

"Car that nice, why would the manager want some kid like you—no offense—to wait on it?"

"I'll get to that," I say, and continue at my own good speed. "First thing I did was stop at the outside washbasin and wash my hands with Lava soap. The car was so shiny I didn't want to get any fingerprints on it."

"Who was driving it?"

"A stocky fellow wearing a black Dutch-boy cap and fine black leather gloves."

"A chauffeur?" the drummer says.

"That's right, a shofer. The shofer gets out right away and sort of inspects me. Then finally he says, 'Ten gallons of high-test, kid, and be careful about it.'

" 'Yessir,' I say. He takes the gas cap off himself, which is helpful because my hands are a little shaky. But soon enough I get the gas running. He don't seem to mind that we got the brand-new kind of pumps where you can't see the actual gasoline anymore; you got to trust the dial. It's the old farmers who still want to see that big glass jar fill up on top the pump with their ten gallons and then watch it empty into their tanks."

"Sure, kid, sure," the drummer sighs. "I been at a few gas stations in my life."

"Anyway, as I'm working I smell cigar smoke coming from the backseat of the car. There's somebody inside smoking the finest stogie I ever smelled, except I can't see him because of the window curtains. So I crane my neck to get a better look, and the shofer says, 'What you rubbernecking at, kid?' 'Nothing, sir,' I say, and hunker back down. Which is when my eyes fall to the left rear tire. There's something small and glinty on the face of it. I take a closer look; it's the head of a nail—looks to be at least a sixteen-penny—which means that tire's gonna go flat sometime real soon."

"And then what?" the drummer asks quickly. I realize we been driving for quite a few miles already now. Funny how a story makes the time pass.

"So I say, 'Sir, there might be a problem with your left rear tire.'

" 'I'll be the judge of that,' he growls, and grabs me by the collar. I almost wished I hadn't said anything, but that was my job, right?"

"Sure, kid, sure."

"So I show him the nail head. He bends down, gives it a good look, then swears a blue streak. 'Is it through the cords?' he asks. I spit on a finger, then dab a nice clear gob around the nail head; little air bubbles start to pop. The shofer swears louder this time, which is when the window rolls down and another voice says, 'Something wrong, Jimmy?'

"I look up and see the man smoking the cigar. He has

brown eyes and wears a porkpie hat. His hat and his cigar cost more than most people's cars.

"'The kid here spotted a nail in the tire,' the shofer says. 'Woulda gone flat just down the road.'

"The door swings open, and the man's shoes come out—leather shined black as oiled walnut. Then his pants cuffs, ironed sharp as a carpenter's square. Gold watch fob on a white shirt. A silk tie. The man was about my father's age, but he was dressed better than Calvin Coolidge himself. He smelled good, too, kinda like mint or toilet water cologne. 'Nice work, son,' he says to me. He pulls out a roll of greenbacks thick enough to choke a horse, then peels off a sawbuck and tucks it into my shirt pocket. I couldn't believe it: ten whole bucks just for spotting a nail."

"Big spender," the salesman murmurs.

"'Can we make it back home on that tire, Jimmy?' the boss man says to the shofer. At the same time he's checking the gold pocket watch. You got the feeling here's a man who don't like surprises.

"'I don't think so, Mr. K,' the shofer says, and turns to me. He gives me another look up and down. 'You ever fixed a Pierce-Arrow tire, kid?' he says.

"'No, sir,' I say, 'but a tire's a tire. Yours looks to be a thirty-two-by-five-point-seventy-seven-inch balloon.'

"'So you think you can handle it?' Mr. K asks me directly.

"I swallow. 'Yessir,' I say.

"Behind me, from the back room, I hear Bob let out a groan, and then the back door slams. I'm on my own now.

"'I don't want no cheap cold patch,' the shofer growls. 'This ain't no bicycle tire.'

" 'Hot-patch vulcanize,' I say. 'It's the only way to fix a tire, sir.'

"The shofer looks to his boss, who nods. 'Go ahead, son,' the boss man says."

"And?" the salesman says impatiently.

"I'm a little nervous, I'll tell you, jacking up the axle and getting the lug nuts off the wheel without rounding off the heads or scratching the fender—the shofer watches me like a vulture—but after I get the tire into the back room, I feel more at home. I lube the bead all around, then slip a pry bar under it and spin off the tire. I turn the inside cords up to the lightbulb. 'There it is,' I say, pointing to the sharp end of the nail. Sometimes I feel kind of like a doctor or scientist or someone like that when I'm fixing a tire. You know what I mean?"

"Kind of, kid, kind of," the salesman mutters.

"Anyway, I dry off the tube, rough up the puncture area with my hand rasp, then get ready with my glue, patch, and matches. The clear glue goes on first; then I crack off the head of a stick match with one thumbnail and touch the flame to the glue. I like that part, how the flame flares up yellow, then dies down to a low blue flicker—which is when I quick lay on the rubber boot with the other hand, then lean on it with a roller to make sure there ain't no air pockets under the rubber."

"Geez, kid, everybody knows how to boot a tire!" the salesman says.

"But some people are better at it than others," I say, and give him a look.

He shrugs and keeps driving.

"Anyway, when I finish putting the tire back together, I

put it in the dunk tank and turn it around and around in the water, but not one air bubble shows. Jimmy the shofer says, 'Nice work, kid.' He turned to his boss, who had been leaning in the doorway all the while, smoking and watching. 'The kid's all right,' Jimmy said.

"The boss nodded. 'And you keep a nice back room, too, son,' he says.

" 'Thank you, sir,' I said. And it was true. You could eat dinner off my tool bench. The PureOil Station had the cleanest back room in town."

"Anyway," the drummer prods.

"Well. After they drive off—me with a second sawbuck tucked in my pocket—Bob comes slinking back into the station. I'm mad as all get-out for him leaving me in the lurch, but what can I say? He's the boss. 'Do you know who that was?' he says. 'Do you know whose tire you just fixed?'

" 'No,' I mutter.

" 'That was Kid Cann Langenfeld.' "

The drummer sits up straighter all at once—but doesn't say anything.

" 'Who's Kid Cann Langenfeld?' I say to my boss.

" 'Don't you know anything?' my boss says to me, beginning to laugh like crazy. 'Kid Cann is a gangster.'

" 'A gangster!' I say. It was like he had punched me in the gut.

" 'Big-time bootlegger. He's killed many a man in Chicago,' my boss adds.

" 'Well, what's a gangster doing way up north in Minnesota?' I say. I'm kinda shaky.

"My boss is laughing now like I'm the dumbest cluck in the coop. 'He's got a lake place north of town. Big estate, all fenced. Everybody knows about it. It ain't like Kid Cann's on the most-wanted list or nothing—at least now. He just pays people off, and when the heat is on, he skedaddles over the border into old Canady.' "

"I hear they do that," the salesman murmurs; he glances in his rearview mirror, then takes a long draw on his cigarette.

"Anyway, I say kinda stubborn-like, 'Mr. Langenfeld seemed nice enough to me.' That's 'cause my daddy always taught me to give a person a chance until he proves you wrong, and—"

"Sure, kid, but you still ain't said—"

"That's where it all started!" I say suddenly to myself. "If I hadn't spotted that nail!"

"Lordy," the drummer says, exasperated. But I don't care. This is my story, not his.

"Anyway, a week later I'm slaving away in the back room fixing a truck tire—the old kind, with a tube—when a horn toots. Bob comes back and says to me, 'Kid, you better hope that Pierce-Arrow tire you fixed didn't go flat.' Then he goes twenty-three skiddoo out the back door. I take a peek. Sure enough, it's the Pierce-Arrow. As I walk to the pumps, I'm so shaky I can hardly put one boot ahead of the next. Jimmy the shofer says, 'Was hoping you were on duty, kid.' My throat is so closed up that all I can squeak is, 'PureOil gas today?'

" 'Naw, that ain't why I'm here,' Jimmy says, friendly-like. 'Mr. K wanted me to ask you something.'

" 'Me?' I say. My mouth goes as dry as steel wool.

" 'Mr. K took a shine to you,' Jimmy says. 'He's looking for a part-time man to do some car work—mainly tires and the like—at his place on the lake. Mr. K is in the wholesale business and has several vehicles. He don't like to come to town all the time, and so he's offering you a job.'

" 'But I got my job here at the PureOil,' I say.

" 'No problem,' Jimmy says. 'This would be after hours. A Saturday here, an evening there.'

" 'I don't know,' I say.

" 'Mr. K will pay triple what you make here.' "

"Triple! Did you take him up on it?" the salesman asks.

I look out across the fields for a brief spell. "Thing of it is, I was up and coming then. That's how I saw myself then. And the money—well, I'd had this wild idea for some time of putting any extra aside toward getting an electrical line run to the farm. A surprise for my folks. Lots of farmers are doing that, paying for a branch line themselves so they can finally have juice. Can't you imagine the look on my folks' faces when they realized that power and light was coming?"

"Sure, kid, sure," the salesman mutters. "But did you take the job?"

"And that gangster business? How was I to know if it was true? Like I say, you gotta give people a chance. I started the next Saturday afternoon. I didn't tell my folks about the extra job—I didn't want my ma to worry—and besides, I wanted that power line to be a surprise. So I just told her I was on extra duty at the PureOil."

"What was his place like? Kind of a mansion, or what?" the salesman says, real interested now. I notice also that the more interested he gets, the faster he drives. We've been buzzing through small towns like a bumblebee through a pumpkin patch on the Fourth of July.

"Not really a mansion," I say. "Just a nice big old log home and a bunch of garages. 'Course, at first all I saw was a tall wooden fence; you couldn't see anything, even from the lake. That fence gave me a shaky feeling, I can tell you. Jimmy musta noticed, 'cause he said, 'Mr. K likes his privacy.'

" 'Yessir,' I said.

" 'Working for Mr. K means you respect that privacy,' Jimmy said as he swung open the iron gate.

" 'Yessir,' I said.

" 'That means you do your work and that's that,' he said. 'Anybody poking their nose into Mr. K's business, you tell me and I'll deal with them. Got that?'

" 'Yessir,' I said. And I went to work right away. First I had to clean up the main shop, which had been let go real bad. There were plenty of mechanic's tools and equipment around, almost as much as at the PureOil station, 'cept it was scattered all over everywhere. Took me two Saturdays to get the shop shined up and in working order. Jimmy the shofer, he was happy to have me around. 'Myself, I'd sure rather drive a car than work on it,' he said more than once. Mr. Langenfeld had a lot of vehicles, and soon enough I was changing tires and spark plugs and adjusting carburetors and all whatnot."

"How many cars?" the salesman interrupts.

"Six, give or take a couple," I said.

"What kind?"

"All the same, basic Model A's, including a couple of trucks."

"Trucks," the salesman says, sly-like. "So what was in them trucks?"

"Nothing," I say right back to him. "No car or truck I worked on ever had anything in them." I don't say that the Model A's—the trucks in particular—smelled kind of strong in back, like green silage juice or sour corn mash for the hogs. But maybe it was vinegar or turpentine, I told myself. And besides, what business was it of mine? "So I just did my job," I continue. "Mr. Langenfeld paid me even better than Jimmy said. The extra money was building up real nice. Things were just fine—until the new sheriff came nosing around."

"New sheriff, you say?" the drummer asks. Funny how certain things seem to interest him.

"Younger guy named Jones, Randall Jones. Beat out Sheriff Anderson in the election last year; said he wasn't tough enough on Prohibition. Found a whiskey still in somebody's barn and made a big enough fuss about it to win the election."

"Lot of them do-gooders around these days," the salesman mutters.

I give him a look.

" 'Course, it all depends on what you think about Prohibition, I guess, don't it?" the salesman says.

I shrug. "My folks don't drink and neither do I. So Prohibition don't matter one way or another to me."

"Well, it matters to a lot of people," the salesman says, giving me a sideways look.

"That's kinda what Mr. Langenfeld said," I continue. "One day he came out into the garage to finish his stogie. When I was working he did that quite a bit, actually. At first I got nervous when he just sat there watching me and smoking, but then I realized he kinda liked the shop the way I ran it, all sharp and tidy. And maybe he needed the company, too; I never saw his wife or kids, though Jimmy said he had a family back East somewhere. So I'd work and we'd talk some—mainly him talking and me listening."

"Well, what'd he have to say?" the salesman asks, leaning toward me slightly.

"One time Mr. Langenfeld asked me the same question—what I thought about Prohibition—and I told him pretty much the same thing: It didn't matter one way or another to me. I told him what my pa said—if people want to take a drink on occasion, and if they don't get drunk and run over someone or burn down their own house and family, then they ought to be left alone. That set him off on a talking jag. He said that it was funny how politicians seemed to get stupid when they got in office—that the country would be better off with farmers like my father running the country. He asked me just how it was the politicians and coppers thought they could change human nature."

"Human nature?" the salesman murmurs.

"He said that people have been drinking and gambling and the like ever since Adam and Eve. He was really wound by then—his cigar was puffing like a steam tractor. 'And no laws will change human nature, which is why Prohibition is bound to fail,' he said."

"He's got a point there," the salesman says.

" 'Politicians are two-faced on Prohibition anyway,' Mr. K said. 'They never did pass any laws against *using* alcohol—just making and selling it.' "

"True again, kid," the salesman observes.

" 'And after Prohibition ends, a few years down the road something else will come along—something on the order of alcohol but maybe worse,' Mr. Langenfeld said, 'and then we'll go through some other kind of Prohibition all over again.' "

We both think about that for a spell as the Packard speeds along.

"He ain't stupid, Kid Cann," the driver murmurs.

I never thought so either, which makes me feel even worse for what happened.

"So, tell me about that sheriff."

I watch a few fence posts pass; I realize I'm getting to the sad part of my story. "One day the new sheriff comes around the PureOil station. Comes right into the back room and wants to talk to me. 'What about?' I say. He says, 'I been watching some of our local citizens, and that includes you, kid.' He's giving me the evil eye by then, and I'm starting to go cotton-mouthed even though I ain't done anything wrong. He says, 'I know you been working out at Kid Cann's place 'cause I seen that shofer pick you up here at the station.'

" 'So? It's a free country,' I said right back. Which was a mistake, because he got all puffed up. 'I also know that your folks don't know about your second job,' he said. 'Do you think they'd like to hear their son is working for a known gangster?' "

"Hard-boiled!" the salesman murmured.

" 'So what do you do for Kid Cann, mow lawns?' the sheriff said.

" 'I do car work,' I said right back.

" 'Car work—I see,' the sheriff says. Then I realize I shouldn't have said anything because that's when the sheriff puts the heat on me. He says he's dead certain that Kid

Cann is bootlegging whiskey, and if anyone was ever man enough to arrest him, that I could be charged with being an accomplice—that I could go to the state pen along with Kid Cann just for working on his cars."

The salesman whistles under his breath.

"I got the shakes then," I say. "The sheriff kept after me for a whole hour until I agreed to help him."

"Help him how?"

"By spying on Mr. Langenfeld," I say bitterly.

The driver looks at me and shakes his head sad-like. "And?"

Truly, my eyes are starting to burn and well up, and I have to watch a full mile of fence posts wing by before I can speak. "Anyway, me and Mr. Langenfeld were getting to be friends by then—at the same time as I'm ratting on him."

"Tough," the salesman says.

"Finally I couldn't take any more. I told Mr. Langenfeld that my grades in school were slipping, and that since I wanted to go to college, I needed those extra hours to study, and that I had to quit." I let out a sharp breath. "What a lie that was."

"And then?" the salesman says.

"Here's the worst part," I say. "Mr. Langenfeld had a going-away party for me. A big shindig in the main house. Jimmy and some of the other drivers and their gals—everybody was there. They all agreed I was going to make something of myself someday. There was even a cake with my name on it, and jazz music on a Victrola record player, plus a champagne toast—apple cider for me, because Mr. Langenfeld didn't want me to learn any bad habits." My voice breaks.

"It's all right, kid. Just get to the punch line," the salesman says.

I gather my wits. "The whole time, and I swear to God I didn't know this, the sheriff and his deputies are sneaking up on the house."

"Geez!" the salesman says.

"And right when they were all singing 'For he's a jolly good fellow,' that's when—"

But suddenly the salesman curses. "Shut up, kid," he says as he slows the Packard and stares into the rearview mirror. I look behind. There's a police car with a flashing red light; then we both hear the siren. "Listen up," the salesman says rapidly as he brakes to a stop. "I got stuff in them trunks under that blanket in the backseat that could get me—and maybe you, too—in a heap of trouble. There's a sawbuck in it for you if you pretend you're my son."

"Your son!"

"Shut up and listen. Here's our story: You're a college boy. We're taking you back to the university in Minneapolis. You been home for a few days, and you need to get back to study for a big test tomorrow. That's why we were speeding—you got that?"

I don't have time to reply; by then a cop is walking up to the Packard.

The salesman rolls down his window and smiles. "Afternoon, Officer. What seems to be the trouble?"

"I don't have any trouble, but you sure do. You was going way too fast through town back there. I clocked you at over fifty miles per hour in the city limits."

"Well, I'll be," the salesman says. "Me and my boy

here—he's in college now—we were just talking up a blue streak because he don't get home that often."

The cop gives me a good looking-over.

"In fact, he's got a big test tomorrow and has to get into the library before it closes," the salesman says.

" 'Zat so?" the cop says.

I nod. "Yessir," I say. What else could I do?

The copper's eyes fall to the trunks in the backseat. "What's in the trunks?"

There is silence. The salesman gives me a sharp kick with his shoe.

"Just my stuff, sir," I say. "Some food. And some winter clothes."

"Well, it's nice you get home to see your folks," the cop says, warming up now, "but we still don't want cars going through our town at high speed."

By then the salesman has pulled out a card. "Here's my driver's license, if that's any use to you," he says. As he hands it over to the policeman, I see a flash of green underneath it.

The policeman takes the license, turns away to write something down, then leans back into the window. "Just take it a little slower next time." He hands back the license—minus the greenback—and salutes.

"Yessir, I'll take it slower next time," the salesman says. He tucks the license back into his shirt pocket, and we drive on.

As the copper recedes, the salesman turns to me. "Nice work, kid. You saved my butt. Here." He pushes a ten-dollar bill across the seat.

"I don't want your damn money," I say suddenly. I set my jaw and stare down the road.

"Hey, you might need it," the salesman says. "See what a little cash did for that cop? He let me off. It's a lesson you gotta learn, kid: Grease the wheels, and the world turns your way."

"Let me out."

"What?"

"I said let me out here, I want to walk."

"Here? There is no here." He gestures to the open fields and fences stretching out of sight ahead.

"I don't care, I want to walk."

He shrugs and pulls over. I get out. "Well, at least let me give you something. In case you get cold later, this will warm you up." He chuckles as he reaches into the backseat under the blanket and pulls out a brown, narrow bottle. "Here!"

I catch it, out of instinct, so the glass doesn't break. And then with a scatter of pebbles and dust, the Packard heads off—but only for a few yards. He brakes suddenly, then backs up. "Hey—you never did tell me who got killed."

"It's none of your beeswax!" I shout at him. I'm suddenly so mad that I haul back that bottle to pitch it at him. The Packard speeds off for good this time.

I stand there in the dust, my arm cocked to throw, but I don't. I lower the bottle and unscrew its cap. I take a whiff. Whew! It's the same sharp smell as in Mr. Langenfeld's truck. Liquor, sure enough. I guess I suspected deep down that those vehicles I worked on all hauled bootleg booze.

Since I am already the scum of the earth, I put the bottle to my lips and take a sip—then spew it out and cough like crazy. It's the vilest stuff I've ever tasted. I can't imagine how adults actually drink this. I let that whiskey *glug-glug* onto the dirt, then pitch the flask hard into the ditch. It shatters into a thousand pieces.

I walk on down the empty road. I keep seeing Jimmy, how he drew a pistol when the door caved forward and the sheriff's boys stormed the place; how he got off a wild shot but took a shotgun blast square in the chest. The noise, the screaming, people diving under tables and things breaking—it was terrible. The sheriff kept hollering, "Don't shoot the boy—he's our pigeon, he's our pigeon!"

And then suddenly it was quiet, except for Jimmy's moaning and gurgling. He died right there on the floor.

The cops went for Mr. Langenfeld and didn't even bother with Jimmy. Maybe even worse was the look on Mr. Langenfeld's face—the way he stared at Jimmy and then at me. It wasn't anger but a sadness in his eyes. He tried to say something to me, but they wrestled him out the door before he could finish.

And I'll never know what he tried to say. On the way to jail, Mr. Langenfeld got killed, too. An escape attempt, the lawmen said. Drew a hidden pistol, they said.

But I don't believe it.

In fact, I don't believe in much of anything right now.

Which is why I'm on the road. If you see me passing through your town or down your street, dusty and all alone, and if you can spare a dime for a bowl of soup, I thank you. But if you've got the answer as to why people do the things they do to each other, all the better. I'm listening. I'm all ears.

Will Weaver

Striking Out, Will Weaver's first novel for teenagers, describes the hard life endured by thirteen-year-old Billy Baggs on a midwestern farm. With a demanding father and too much work, Billy's life begins to change when he starts playing baseball and discovers his talent for pitching. Because he grew up in rural Minnesota, Weaver's knowledge of farm life is realistic and vividly described, from the smells of the animals to the dangers of farm machinery.

Billy's experiences continue in *Farm Team* as he develops his pitching arm and makes friends—as well as enemies—when he meets baseball players from town. However, with his hotheaded father in jail, Billy finds himself responsible for running the family farm. There is little time for recreation until he and his always optimistic mother construct a baseball field on their land. They organize their own "farm team," a motley group including two Mexican boys, a mentally handicapped neighbor, two foul-mouthed sisters, a Jewish city kid, and a dog in center field. But the Farm Team players are no laughing matter, as the local team soon discovers.

Both *Striking Out* and *Farm Team* were American Library Association Best Books for Young Adults as well as New York Public Library Books for the Teen Age, and have been included on the Iowa and Texas Teen Award Lists for schools.

Hard Ball, the most recent in the Billy Baggs series, finds Billy getting ready for ninth grade, where he hopes to star on the high-school baseball team. But first he must deal with a challenge from his town rival, King Kenwood, his father's continuing anger, and the distraction caused by Suzy Langen, the most beautiful girl in the ninth grade. _Hard Ball_ was a 1999 ALA Best Book for Young Adults.

Will Weaver lives in Bemidji, Minnesota, where he teaches creative writing at Bemidji State University. He has also published a collection of short stories, _A Gravestone Made of Wheat_, and a novel, _Red Earth, White Earth_, both for adults. That novel was made into a television movie that aired on CBS. He is currently finishing a new young adult novel about one family's survival in a world-class natural disaster.

For more information about Will Weaver's work, and for his recommendations of other authors who write for young adults, take a look at his Web site at www.cal.bemidji.msus.edu.EnglishClub/Weaver.html.

1930 - 1939

In contrast to the exuberance of the 1920s, the 1930s were quite grim. The collapse of the stock market at the end of 1929 resulted in a worldwide financial crisis and the worst economic depression America has ever experienced. Conditions worsened when droughts and dust storms in the plains states destroyed many farms. And when the drought ended, millions of people were left homeless by floods in the Midwest in 1937.

In the rest of the world, civil war erupted in Spain, Italy invaded North Africa, Japan invaded eastern China, the Soviets invaded Finland, and Adolf Hitler and his Nazi party rose to power in Germany and then annexed Austria, took over Czechoslovakia, and invaded Poland.

In spite of all that negativity, life went on in several positive ways. Perhaps to forget their problems for a while, Americans flocked to theaters to see musicals, such as *Anything Goes*, and films, such as *Frankenstein*,

King Kong, The Wizard of Oz, and *Gone with the Wind.*
Nylon, aluminum foil, acrylic plastics, Teflon, and the jet
engine were invented. And as the economy improved,
household appliances—including vacuum cleaners,
washing machines, and refrigerators with freezer com-
partments—became more plentiful.

But the most enduring images of the 1930s are of
the Great Depression, during which nearly one-fourth
of the working population was unemployed and the
average income of working Americans was less than
half of what it had been in 1929. Thousands of people
stood in lines waiting for donations of food each day,
and people looked for work wherever they could find it.
To understand what life was like during the Great
Depression, a present-day fictional teenager interviews
an old man who had been a teenager in rural
Massachusetts during the thirties and submits the following report about his memories.

Brother, Can You Spare a Dream?

by Jackie French Koller

Lisa Bridges, English 12, Amherst High School
Oral History Project: The Great Depression
Subject: Samuel Fowler, age 80, Amherst, MA
Visit #3—April 19, 2000

It was a mild spring day when I stopped in for my third visit with Sam Fowler. We sat in the kitchen of his small farmhouse in Amherst and he made us both a cup of tea. Sam has Parkinson's disease, which makes his hands tremble and causes him to move with a slow, shuffling step. His mind is sharp, though, and he still manages to look after his house and care for himself. He has a raspy voice and an old-time Yankee accent. Sam and I spent my first two visits getting to know each other, and by the third, we were on a first-name basis despite the difference in our ages. Sam often talked about missing his wife, May, who had died two years earlier, and I think he had come to look forward to my visits. I felt it was time to press forward with the project.

"As you know, Sam," I said, "I'm studying the Great Depression. Would you mind telling me in your own words what it was like for you?"

Sam rubbed his white-whiskered chin a moment, then sat back in his chair. "Well," he said, "I lived in the Swift River Valley then, y'know, and for us the Depression come early. Boston was outgrowin' her water supply, y'see, and lookin' for someplace to plant a new reservoir, and before you know it there were rumors about the valley. It had everything Boston was lookin' for—plenty of water, a perfect bowl shape, and all it needed were two small dams at its southern end to turn it into a reservoir big enough for Boston to drown in.

"Valley folks thought the rumors were just nonsense at first. Boston was sixty-five miles away, don't forget. But the rumors kept up, and then surveyor's stakes were found in places where they had no business bein', and at last, on a mornin' in 1919, the valley folks picked up their newspapers and read, 'Swift River Doomed!'

"Well, that was the beginnin' of the end. Property values fell, and businesses packed up and left. People started leavin', too, but lots of 'em, like my folks, found themselves trapped in homes that wouldn't sell. When the Swift River Act finally passed in the late twenties, the Metropolitan District Water Supply Commission began buyin' up the properties, but the values had fallen so by then that many folks could hardly pay off their mortgages with the money they got. It was the beginnin' of the Depression and folks had nowhere to turn, so the commission decided to let them lease back their properties and stay on until the dams were built."

"Is that what your folks did?" I asked.

"Yep," said Sam. "The leases they offered were dirt cheap. We got our farm, includin' outbuildings and eighty acres of land, for five dollars a month. That's how we managed to keep our family together and ride out the worst of the Depression."

"Tell me a little about your life in those days," I asked him.

Sam took a sip of his tea, gripping the cup with both hands. "Oh, we were poor. We had no 'lectricity, runnin' water, phone . . . no nothing. And our clothes were patched, and patched, and patched some more. When we outgrew 'em, my ma would cut down somethin' of hers for my younger sister, Kate, or somethin' of Pa's for me. Or sometimes she'd get hand-me-downs from a neighbor or the church, and then she'd make 'em over to fit us.

"Bein' farmers, we always had food, though. We had a milk cow and a coupla chickens, and Pa grew corn and tomatas, pumpkins and beans. We had blueberry bushes and apple trees, so there were always pies 'n' cobblers, and come spring we'd tap the maple trees and make maple-sugar candy. That was our favorite. We had plenty to keep us busy, too—fields to roam and berries to pick, brooks to splash in and trees to climb. And we had community. Do you know what I mean b'that?"

I shrugged.

Sam sighed, like he'd expected as much. "You young folks today don't know what you're missin'," he said. "We were such a small town, y'see, that everybody knew everybody. We had hay rides and sleigh rides, birthday parties, huskin' bees, town picnics, church suppers . . . And we kids went to everything, even the grange hall dances, which we loved, because the grown-ups always got tipsy, don't you know, and we'd sneak around taking sips out of their glasses when they weren't lookin'." Sam chuckled at the memory.

"Then we'd all dance," he went on, "or more like it— trip over each other's feet—to all the old big-band tunes. Now that was music—Tommy Dorsey, Glenn Miller . . . I remember the 'Beer Barrel Polka' come out 'round that time, and that was a big favorite. Didn't we tear up the floor to that one!"

"It seems that the Depression didn't have too bad an effect on you, then," I said.

"Well, when we got to be teenagers, it was differ'nt, of course. We went up to the high school in Athol then, and we started to care how we looked, you know? Kate got into readin' those movie-star magazines, and natur'ly she wanted to be glamorous like Greta Garbo or Marlene Dietrich. And I started noticin' girls. I remember one day I was walkin' down Main Street and a girl called out my name. I think I was about sixteen at the time. Well, I turned around, and wasn't it Emma Bradley! What a pretty little thing she was. . . ."

Sam looked at me. "I hope you don't take offense at that, me callin' her a pretty little thing. I know young women these days take offense at that sort of thing some-times. I don't know why. Times are changing so's I hardly understand 'em anymore."

I smiled. "No offense taken, Sam. Go on."

"Well, she was about the prettiest girl in the eleventh grade—cute little figure, and eyes as green as apples in July. I was so surprised to hear her call my name that I turned clear around to see if maybe there wasn't some other Sam standin' behind me."

"Sam," I said with a laugh, "give yourself credit."

Sam laughed. "Oh, I wasn't much to look at. I'm sure she was just bein' neighborly, callin' my name like that. But you know how young boys are. I took it for a sign that maybe she was sweet on me, and that was it. I was smitten. I spent the rest of that school year moonin' over her. I'd try to second-guess where she was gonna be next so I could be there first, you know? I'd toss a ball against the wall or pretend to be readin' a book, just hopin' she'd call my name again. But she never did. And that's when I b'gan to realize how nice it would be to have a little money.

"See, there were boys in town that did have money. They were the sons of the engineers and construction workers that'd moved to the valley to work on the dams. I remember this one fella, Tommy Cruthers. He took Emma into Athol to see *Les Misérables*. That was the big picture that year. Then there was this other fella, Dennis somethin' er other. He had enough money to buy a Monopoly game. Monopoly was brand-new back then, you know, and everybody was talkin' about it. Well, of course he bought it and invited Emma over to play, and didn't she go on and on about it in school the next day and let Dennis walk her home.

"And then I remember another lad. I think his name was Michaels. Uh . . . David, yes, David Michaels. Well, he went out and bought a copy of *Gone with the Wind*, which had just come out and was all the rage, and he would sit with Emma on a park bench after school and read it to her. If you could see how she used to look into his eyes while he was readin' . . . Well, it near broke my heart, of course, stuck on her the way I was, and I began to scheme how I could get some money, too, so's I could take Emma out and show her a good time."

"Did you have any luck?" I asked.

"Well," said Sam, "the funny thing was, b'fore long an announcement showed up in the local paper. It said that three thousand men were to be hired over the summer to begin clearin' the reservoir basin of brush and trees, and they were to be paid four dollars a day. Now, I'll tell you, four dollars a day was a fortune! My whole family was lucky if we could scrape together four dollars in a *week*. Well, I made up my mind right then and there that I was gonna be first in line when that employment office opened, believe you me.

"Only the employment office never opened—not for us valley folks, anyway. Instead, we got word that Governor Curley was handing out the jobs to Boston men, and that these woodpeckers, as we soon nicknamed them, were to be bused into the valley for the summer. Valley folks were being asked to put 'em up in return for a few dollars' room and board. Well, I don't mind tellin' you I was sore as a wet hen.

" 'That ain't fair!' I remember complainin' to my parents. 'We're not gonna take in any of them woodpeckers, are we?'

" 'Three dollars a week is better than none,' my ma said. And that was that. Next thing I knew, one of them woodpeckers come knockin' on our door. That's quite an interestin' story, actually. I remember it like yesterday."

Sam paused and looked at me. "That's the funny thing

about getting old. Somethin' happened fifty years ago, you remember so clear, and somethin' happened only yesterday . . . Well, never mind.

"Like I was sayin', I come in for supper one night, and the whole kitchen smelled like Ma's maple baked beans. You could always tell summer was on the way when Ma started bakin' beans. She and Kate made extra money peddlin' them off the back of our truck every summer to the folks up on Greenwich Lake.

"Anyway, a knock come on the door this night, and there stood this city slicker with a lumpy old satchel in one hand. He was short and thin, dressed kind of shabby—but then, I was one to talk—and he coulda used a shave and a haircut. He reached out a hand to me. 'Name's Mike McGovern,' he said. 'I'm—'

" 'Know who you are,' I told him, and I ignored his hand. That wasn't very polite, I know. But the way I saw it, this fella had stole my job, and I was pretty burned up about it.

"Ma come bustling over and welcomed him in. 'Kate,' she said, 'set another place for our guest.'

" '*Guest?*' I said, givin' the woodpecker a dirty look. 'I thought he was a *boarder.*'

"Well, Ma shot me a look fit to kill, and I knew I'd better mind my manners. As I recall, Kate was pretty mad at me, too. 'Don't mind him none,' she told the woodpecker. 'He's just ignorant.'

"Well, she and I went at it a little bit, the way kids do, till my pa walked in. One look at his face told us he was in no mood for shenanigans.

" 'Something wrong?' Ma asked him.

" 'The tractor,' Pa muttered. 'Starter's gone.'

" 'Oh, dear,' said Ma.

"Everyone was quiet for a moment, and then the woodpecker stepped forward. 'Mike McGovern, sir,' he said, putting out his hand. 'Folks call me Mac. I guess I'll be boardin' with you awhile.'

"I don't think Pa had noticed him till then, and he looked a little embarrassed. He didn't like outsiders to know our troubles. But he played over it. 'Welcome, Mac,' he said, shaking the woodpecker's hand. 'Sit down, please.'

"Pa took his usual seat at the head of the table and offered grace. Mac folded his hands in front of him, and I couldn't help but notice how soft and smooth they were. I doubted he'd ever swung an ax in his life.

"Ma started passing around the platters of food, and Mac filled his plate and dug in like a half-starved cur. I didn't do much talkin', but Ma and Pa and Kate chatted with Mac as they ate. The conversation eventually come 'round to the reservoir.

" 'How do folks around here feel about the whole thing?' Mac asked.

" 'How do *you* think?' I grumbled.

"Kate gave me a sharp look, then smiled at Mac. 'I, for one, can't *wait* to leave,' she said. 'The valley has gotten so dull. We don't even have our own picture show anymore.'

"Pa cleared his throat. 'Most of us don't see it quite like Kate does,' he told Mac. 'Truth is, we're angry. This valley's our home. Been home to some for generations. We feel we got a raw deal.'

" 'Yeah,' I added, 'and we're still gettin' it. They

promised us jobs, and instead they go out and bring you city slickers in.'

"There was an awkward silence, and then Mac turned to me. 'I'm sorry about that,' he said, 'but it's not my doin'. The job was offered, and I took it. Reckon you'da done the same.'

"He was right, of course. I would've done exactly the same. But that didn't make me like him or the whole situation one bit better.

" 'Enough about us,' Ma said, frowning at me. 'Why don't you tell us about yourself, Mac?'

"Mac paused with a forkful of beans halfway to his mouth.

" 'Ain't much to tell,' he said.

" 'How about your family?' asked Ma.

" 'Got none,' said Mac.

" 'Oh, I'm sorry,' said Ma. 'You live with friends, then?'

"Mac shook his head. 'No, ma'am,' he said. 'I'm on my own.'

"Kate's eyes lit up at that. 'Keen,' she said.

"Mac glanced at her. 'Being on your own ain't all it's cracked up to be,' he told her. 'I wouldn't be in such a big hurry for it if I were you.'

"Kate colored up. 'You would if you lived in *this* town,' she mumbled.

" 'If you don't mind my asking,' said Ma, 'how old are you, Mac?'

" 'Seventeen. Just graduated twelfth grade.'

" 'Ever done land clearin' before?' Pa asked.

"Mac laughed. 'I'm afraid there's not much uncleared land in Boston,' he said. 'I've run errands, shined shoes, peddled papers, hauled ice—earned a buck just about any way I could. Last few years it's been tough, though. Grown men'll fight you for any job these days.'

" 'Still,' said Kate, 'it must be so excitin' to live in a big city. I'll bet there's a picture show on every corner. Hey! Maybe I can come visit you when you get back.'

"Ma just about dropped her teeth at that. 'Kathleen Fowler, I declare!' she cried.

" 'Don't worry,' Mac told her. 'I'm not *goin'* back. Soon as this job's done I'm heading to Ohio. Got me a scholarship to college out there.'

" 'Hotsy totsy!' said Kate. 'A college man!'

"Well, that did it. Ma plunked her glass down on the table, sloshing water all over the place. 'Kathleen Fowler!' she said. 'To your room. Now!'

"Well, Kate jumped up and put on a big show of falling on her knees by Ma's chair and beggin' forgiveness. She always was dramatic like that, and being the youngest, and a girl, she could get away with just about anything. Next thing you know, Pa was chucklin' into his napkin and Ma was throwing her hands up.

" 'Oh, very well,' she told Kate. 'Mind your manners and help me get dessert.'

" 'I really do think it's the bee's knees that you're going to college,' Kate told Mac when she slid back into her chair. 'I'm such a dumb Dora, I'll be lucky if I get through high school. Latin positively gives me fits.'

"Mac smiled. 'Readin' and writin' just come easy to me,' he said. 'I figure college is my ticket out of—' He stopped speaking then, and turned red. I reckon he realized he'd put his foot in his mouth. 'Anyhow, that's why I need this job,' he added quickly. 'To pay my way to Ohio and buy my books.' He finished his pie then and made a show of yawning. 'If you all don't mind,' he said, 'it's been a long day. . . .'

" 'Oh, certainly.' Ma nodded at me. 'Go along and show Mac where he'll be staying, Sam,' she said.

" 'But I'm not done with my pie,' I told her.

" 'I'll take him,' said Kate, jumping up.

"Ma put a hand on Kate's arm and gave me a hard look. 'Sam will take him,' she said. 'Won't you, Sam?'

" 'Yes, ma'am,' I said, but I shoveled the last of my pie into my mouth before I got up."

I asked Sam, "Did Mac stay in the house with your family?"

"Yep," he answered. "Stayed in my room, in fact. I had twin beds, you know, and Ma had cleared out a dresser for him. I remember watchin' as he unpacked his things. He had a few items of clothing and he put those in his top drawer, but mostly what he had was a bunch of beat-up old books. And didn't he treat them like gold, liftin' them out one by one and arranging them on the dresser top.

" 'What're all them books for?' I asked him.

" 'Readin',' he said.

" 'That's a lot of readin',' I told him. 'Must be nice to have that kind of free time.'

"Well, I was just givin' him a hard time, of course, and he knew it, so he didn't answer, which made me all the angrier.

" 'Oh, I forgot,' I said sarcastically. 'Reading is your ticket out of this Depression, ain't it? Must be nice to have one of them tickets. I thought I had one, too. It was called a job. But they gave it to—'

" 'Look,' Mac interrupted, 'I told you I'm sorry about that, but it's not my doing. Now, if you'll just show me where the bathroom is . . .'

"I laughed. 'You'll find it in the backyard,' I told him, 'only we call it a privy. Welcome to the country, city boy.' "

"So they would have had plumbing in the cities back then?" I inquired.

"Oh, sure," said Sam. "That was the mid-thirties. They had plumbing, 'lectricity, everything."

"So Mac was really roughing it living with you?"

Sam chuckled to himself. "Yep. But he was no baby. In fact, I was up at the first cock's crow that next morning, and wasn't that son of a gun's bed empty already! That caught me by surprise, to tell the truth, but I remember thinking to myself, We'll just see if he's such an eager beaver after his first day of real labor.

"Sure enough, he dragged in that evening lookin' worse than a whipped dog. His hands were so blistered that his work gloves were soaked with blood. His face and neck were covered with bug bites. His clothes were all snagged and torn, and the sole of one of his shoes was loose and flapping. He was a mess, all right.

" 'You poor boy,' Ma fretted. 'Go douse yourself at the pump with some nice cool water, then come in and let me tend to those blisters.'

"I have to admit I was gloating a little to myself. At that rate I was sure he wouldn't last another day. He did, though, son of a gun. Next morning he tied his shoe up with an old rag, rubbed a little more of Ma's bag balm into his blisters, and trudged off without a complaint. By the end of the week I had to admit he'd earned my respect. I figured anybody that worked that hard couldn't be all bad. I dug an old pair of boots out of a box in the barn and cleaned the dirt and mildew off of them as best I could.

" 'Here,' I said when he got home that night. 'Your feet look a little smaller than mine. If these fit, you can have 'em.'

"Well, he wanted them all right. That was plain. But he didn't reach for 'em right away. Pride held him back, I s'pose.

" 'Boots were just rotting out there in the barn,' I told him. 'Ain't no big deal.'

"He hesitated a little longer, then he swallowed his pride and sat right down and pulled 'em on. They seemed to fit fair enough. He looked up and gave me an embarrassed smile. ' 'Preciate it,' he said quietly.

"I nodded and walked away. No use makin' him feel any worse, you know?"

"That was really nice of you," I said.

Sam looked down. "Just common decency is all," he muttered; then he took another sip of tea.

"That must be cold," I said. "Can I heat it up for you?"

"No, no," said Sam. "I don't much like tea, t'be honest. It's just somethin' to sip. May used to make a good pot of coffee, and I liked that. My doctor won't let me have coffee no more, though." He shook his head. "Terrible thing, getting old." He looked over at the stove and seemed to drift off.

"Sam?" I said after a while.

"Yep?" He looked back at me and blushed. "Sorry. Mind wanders sometimes, y'know. Where was I now? Oh, yes, that woodpecker fella. Well, it was about a week after I give him the boots that Pa come hurryin' toward me across the cornfield one day. Even at that distance I could tell somethin' was wrong.

" 'Milk wagon stopped by with bad news,' he told me. 'Mac's been hurt. They got him down to Doc Segur's. Tree fell on him. Busted up his leg pretty bad.'

"I winced. 'Those fool woodpeckers,' I said. 'Be lucky if they don't all kill each other. How bad is he?'

" 'Bone's shattered,' Pa said. 'Doc patched him up, but he's gonna be laid up for some time. You better take the truck down and bring him home.'

"Now, I'm not proud to tell you this, but soon as I heard that he was gonna be laid up awhile, my ears perked up.

" 'Laid up?' I said to Pa. 'How long?'

"Pa scratched his head. 'Coupla months, I'll wager.'

" 'His job'll be open, then,' I said quietly.

"Pa stared at me, chewing on my meaning, and I could see he didn't much like the taste.

" 'If I don't go after it,' I told him, 'someone else will.'

"Pa sighed and nodded. 'Seems a damn lousy thing to do,' he said, 'but you got a point, son. Guess you ought to stop by the commission on your way to the doc's.'

"It was hard telling Mac I'd gotten his job. He laid in his bed there, with his cast propped up on a coupla books, and he just stared at me.

" 'If I didn't go after it, someone else would've,' I told him.

"He dropped his eyes. 'Ain't blaming you,' he said. 'I'da done the same thing.' Then he turned his face to the wall.

"Well, I felt bad for him, but I forgot about it pretty quick when I got my first week's pay. I give half of it to Ma, then I spent the rest on a box of Fannie Farmer chocolates, two tickets to the Fireman's Ball, a bottle of hair tonic, and a new shirt. I rubbed the tonic into my scalp, slicked back my hair, put on the shirt, stuck the tickets in my pocket and the candy under my arm, and marched across town and right up to Emma Bradley's front porch.

"She looked mighty surprised to see me. 'Why, Sam,' she said when I handed her the candy. 'Is this for me?'

" 'Yep,' I told her.

" 'Well, aren't you just the sweetest thing,' she said. Then she stretched right up there on her tiptoes and kissed me on the cheek! Well, I tell you, I was so surprised I lost my balance and nearly fell off the porch. Emma giggled, and darned if I couldn't think of another word to say. We stood there like that, her in the doorway and me staring at her with my mouth hangin' open until at last she asked me if I'd come by for some reason, that is, other than to bring her chocolates.

" 'Oh, yes,' I said, suddenly remembering. I pulled the tickets from my pocket. 'I got these,' I said, 'and I wondered if you—'

" 'Oooh,' she said, cutting me right off. 'I'm sorry, Sam. I'm already going.'

"Well, that knocked the wind out of my sails. 'You are?' I mumbled.

" 'Yes,' she said. 'David Michaels asked me. He's taking

me in his new Packard. Have you seen it? It's just the berries!'

" 'Yep,' I told her as I turned away. 'I've seen it.'

"Well, I can tell you, I walked all the way home kicking a stone and trying to figure out how long it would take me to save up for a car."

I smiled.

"I felt a little guilty when I got home, though, thinkin' how I'd wasted that paycheck, and what that money would've meant to Mac. But then . . . well, you know how easy it is to twist things around in your mind and make them come out the way you want. What did I have to feel guilty about? I asked myself. He got a bad break, that's all. It wasn't my doin'. And after all, my folks were letting him stay on till he was well—giving him room and board for free. That was more than a lot of folks would've done in those times."

"I'm sure that's true," I said.

Sam nodded and stared down into his cold tea. "Didn't really make me feel a whole lot better, though. Mac didn't have much to say to me the whole rest of the summer, but he got on fine with the rest of the family. Soon as he got so's he could hobble around, he insisted on helpin' out wherever he could. He'd feed the chickens, weed Ma's kitchen garden, clean and oil Pa's tools. Ma and Pa and Kate grew right fond of him, but between me and him there just seemed to be a whole briar patch of prickly feelings.

"My wages made a big difference to my family, and I was proud of that. Pa was able to get the new starter for the tractor, and Ma bought some extra chickens and started selling eggs up to Greenwich Lake along with her beans. Kate even got a new dress to wear to the Grange Summer Swing. She invited Mac even though he couldn't dance, and he seemed pleased to go. I asked Emma, but as usual, some other fella was there ahead of me. You'd think I woulda got the hint by then, but I didn't. I had my eye on a little old Maxwell roadster out behind the fillin' station. Each week I put my half of my pay in a cigar box in my top drawer. By the end of the summer I figured I'd have enough to make an offer on it. All day long while I was choppin' trees and brush under the hot sun I cooled myself with daydreams of me and Emma speedin' along in that little Maxwell with the wind blowing through our hair."

"Sounds like fun," I said.

Sam laughed. "Oh, sure, the daydreamin' was fun, but when I come home it'd be a different story. I'd catch sight of Mac hobblin' around the hen yard with his crutch, or shellin' beans on the back porch with his stiff leg straight out in front of him, or propped up in bed, brooding over them books of his, and all my happy thoughts would drain away quick as runoff after a storm."

"But why did you feel so guilty?" I asked. "I don't think I would have."

"Well," said Sam, "there was somethin' else I've yet to mention. See, I'd met a few of Mac's old friends on the job and found out about his life back in Boston. Seems he did have family back there, but it wasn't any wonder he didn't want to talk about 'em. Turned out his pa was in jail for killing some guy in a barroom brawl, and his ma had taken up with a hobo who'd come to her back door looking for a handout. Seems the new boyfriend was somethin' of a boozer, and whenever he tied one on, he'd get ornery and slap Mac around."

"Oh," I said quietly. "No wonder he didn't want to go back there."

"Mmm," said Sam. "I remember askin' along toward August what he was gonna do when he got the cast off, but he didn't answer.

" 'You still heading to Ohio?' I asked.

" 'Don't know,' he said. 'It's a long walk.'

" 'You could hitch, or catch a freight,' I suggested.

" 'Won't do me much good without books.'

"I remember glancing at my top drawer, knowin' I could give Mac his dream back if I wanted. But the thing is, I had a dream of my own by then, and I wasn't about to give it up.

" 'Something'll work out,' I told Mac. 'My ma always says, "Where there's a will there's a way." '

" 'Yeah,' Mac said bitterly. 'I used to believe in fairy tales, too.'

"His cast come off later that month. He still had a pretty bad gimp, and Doc said he always would. The leg had healed shorter than his other one, and there was no help for it."

"Life sure seemed determined to beat the kid down, huh?" I said.

Sam nodded. "That night at supper he told us he'd be leavin' the next day. He was asleep when I left for work, so I didn't get to say goodbye. My conscience weighed heavy on me all day, though. See, I didn't have a lot, but I knew I had a lot more than Mac. I sure coulda used that Maxwell, but Mac . . . Mac sure coulda used a break. I kept goin' back and forth in my mind like that, but by the end of the day I'd managed to convince myself that Mac wasn't my responsibility. I figured if he was tough enough, he'd still make his dream come true somehow. And if not, well, those were the breaks.

" 'Mac gone yet?' I asked Ma when I got home.

" 'He left a couple of hours ago,' she said. 'He said to tell you he'd be in touch.'

"I remember thinking that was odd. After all, we'd hardly even spoken while he was there. Why would he be in touch? I put it down to bein' one of those meaningless things folks say when parting, and I went on up to my room.

"I stared at Mac's bed and at the dresser with all his books gone, and I felt kind of empty. I'd liked him, you see, and I'd thrown away our chance to be friends because of the money. I was angry at myself, and I went over to my top drawer and pulled the cigar box out. I flipped it open and looked inside . . . and danged if it wasn't empty."

"No way!" I said. "He took the money?"

"Yep," said Sam. "Shocked me, too. I dropped the box and ran downstairs.

" 'Which way did he go?' I asked my mother.

" 'Toward town,' she said. 'Why?'

"The bus station, I realized. I ran out of the house and jumped on my bike and pedaled like mad the whole five miles into town. Just as I come over the last rise I saw him dead ahead. The sight of him drew me up short, and I stopped and tried to think what I should do. That's when that message come back to me—the one he'd given my mother. I couldn't help wonderin' if that'd been his way of saying he meant to pay me back someday."

"Even so, that still didn't make it right," I said.

"No. No, it didn't," said Sam. "But you know something? As I stood there, watching him limp along, lugging his lumpy satchel of dreams, I figured out somethin'. I figured out that there was a fine line between need and greed, and that line was right there between me and Mac."

"So what'd you do?" I asked.

"I turned around and rode home."

"Without saying a word?"

"Without saying a word."

"Did you ever hear from him again?" I asked.

"Nope," said Sam, "but we left the valley soon after that. The commission said it was time to go. Kate and I moved in with friends in Athol so's we could finish our schoolin', and my folks went on the road doin' migrant work. Once I finished high school, I joined the Civilian Conservation Corps and moved around quite a lot. So I don't know if Mac ever tried to reach me or not. I like to think he did, though."

Sam looked out the window as though he still expected that Mac might come walking up his front steps any day now.

"Whatever happened with Emma?" I asked.

Sam glanced at me, and his cheeks reddened like a schoolboy's. His eyes flicked in the direction of an old photograph that was stuck to the front of his refrigerator, and a gentle radiance lit his face. "Well," he said softly, "I found May, you see. . . ."

Jackie French Koller

Jackie French Koller's connections with the Great Depression began when she wrote *Nothing to Fear,* a novel based on her mother's memories of growing up in New York City during that time. It's a story about the teenage son of Irish immigrants who tries to help support the family after his father moves away and his mother becomes ill. This novel was an American Library Association (ALA) Best Book for Young Adults as well as an International Reading Association (IRA) Teacher's Choice and a Young Adults' Choices book, and won the Utah Young Adult Book Award in 1996.

Koller's interest progressed further when she began hiking around the Quabbin Reservoir near her home in Westfield, Massachusetts, and saw the remains of old roads and the foundations of old houses. Through research she discovered that four towns used to exist in the Swift River Valley in the 1930s; their remains now lie beneath the waters of the great reservoir. Her interviews with former residents inspired her to begin work on a novel about the last days of those communities, a book she is still working on. In the meantime, Koller has included some of that background in her short story "Brother, Can You Spare a Dream?"

Primrose Way is another of her historical novels, this one set in the seventeenth century. It follows the adventures of the sixteen-year-old daughter of a Puritan missionary in 1633 Massachusetts who is attracted to the ways of the Pawtucket people and especially to the leader Mashannok. The ALA named this a Best Book for Young Adults in 1993.

Jackie French Koller is also the author of *A Place to Call Home*, a novel about a biracial fifteen-year-old girl who has to care for her younger brother and sister when their alcoholic mother abandons them. This inspirational book was an ALA Notable Book, an *American Bookseller* Pick of the Lists, and an IRA Teacher's Choice selection.

Koller's most recent novel for teenagers, another ALA Best Book for Young Adults, is based on a true incident involving her oldest son, Ryan. In *The Falcon*, a reckless and accident-prone seventeen-year-old, while writing a long-term journal assignment for English class, slowly comes to terms with a secret he has been hiding from everyone, including himself.

Besides these books for teenagers, Jackie French Koller has published a novelette for middle-graders called *The Promise*, along with several children's picture books, including a series of Dragonling books, the Mole and Shrew books, *One Monkey Too Many*, *Bouncing on the Bed*, and *Nickommoh! A Thanksgiving Celebration*.

You can find out more about Jackie French Koller by accessing her Web site at www.jackiefrenchkoller.com.

1940 - 1949

World War II dominated almost everyone's life for more than half of the 1940s. Intent on defeating the Nazis in Europe and the Japanese in the Pacific, Americans were encouraged to "use it up, wear it out, or do without." Food was rationed, and anything made of rubber, metal, paper, nylon, or silk was recycled.

In factories and on farms, women took the roles of the men who had gone to war, gaining greater responsibilities and independence. The war was also responsible for the development of guided missiles, as well as nuclear weapons. Answering machines, electronic calculators, computers, microwave ovens, 45-rpm records, and high-fidelity (hi-fi) recordings were also developed during this decade, along with the Polaroid camera, the Frisbee, Velcro fasteners, disposable diapers, the bikini swimsuit, the ballpoint pen, and Scrabble.

At the same time, Colonel Sanders invented his Kentucky Fried Chicken recipe, M&M's (only brown ones) were created for the military, and Richard and Maurice McDonald opened their first drive-in restaurant, in Pasadena, California.

Jackie Robinson and Larry Doby broke the color barrier in professional baseball; Captain Chuck Yeager, in the Bell X-1 rocket plane, broke the sound barrier for the first time; and Joe DiMaggio hit safely in fifty-six consecutive baseball games, a record no one has ever come close to breaking.

The war, nevertheless, had a terrible effect on human lives, killing nearly fifty-five million people throughout Europe, Russia, North Africa, the Pacific, and most notably in the Nazi death camps. In the following story, Graham Salisbury focuses on one afternoon in the life of two teenage boys trying to ride a stubborn horse and one soldier waiting to be called to battle. In the sun-warmed tranquillity of Hawaii, the shadow of death waits . . . just beyond the horizon.

Waiting for the War

by Graham Salisbury

About a mile inland from Pearl Harbor, Henry Long and Sammy Maldonado, two sixteen-year-old island boys, were trying to ride a horse.

Actually, they were trying to catch it.

To Henry, the horse was a menace. It would just as soon kick you in the face as look at you, and Henry was kicking himself for having bought it. But he sure wasn't about to admit that to Sammy.

It was the old forgotten brown horse in the weedy pasture not far from his house. The animal had been in there for as many years as Henry could remember.

Now it was his.

But he couldn't ride it because he couldn't get on it, and he couldn't get on it because he couldn't even catch it. The horse had a mean streak as long as an aircraft carrier.

It nipped him on the shoulder. It stepped on his foot and kicked his shin. Henry couldn't even get a rope over its head, and he was sorry he'd paid any kind of money for it. But Henry had his pride and wasn't about to admit the horse was a mistake.

"The old man ruined it," Sammy told Henry. "Because he never rode it."

"It ain't ruined. It's a good horse."

"What's so good about it? You can't even catch it."

"So. It just needs to get used to me."

"Or maybe it just don't like people. But it looks like a good horse, yeah? Check out its back. Straight, not swayback."

Henry glared at Sammy, who he knew had never been on a horse in his life. "*You* catch it, then. You get on it."

"But I think you could ride it, if you're nice to it."

"*Nice* to it?"

"Yeah. Give it grass, pet it."

"You don't pet horses."

"How come?"

Henry shook his head. "You just don't. You brush it, you slap its side or neck, you give it apples and weeds and comb its mane, but you don't *pet* it. It ain't a dog. It ain't a . . . a . . . cat."

Sammy shrugged.

The horse had belonged to a nice but sly old guy named Wong. "Only eleven years old," he'd said. "Still young yet, like you, Henry. He just jumpy because of the bombs, yeah? Was too close to all those explosions. Even had one went off in this pasture. Over there. See the hole?"

Henry saw the indentation in the grass. That had been a bad day, he remembered. Lot of noise, lot of smoke, planes, police, sirens. Almost two years, now, since the Japanese planes came. Thank goodness it had been only *one* bad day, and lucky the Japanese never landed troops like everyone thought they would. Really lucky.

"You sure you can ride it?" Henry asked Wong.

"Yeah-yeah. Look at him. Strong. Spunky. Got a nice high step. I give you 'um for . . . hmmm . . . fie dollah."

That's what did it. *Five dollars.* For a *horse!* Henry couldn't pass it up.

"But I can only buy it if I can keep it in your pasture," Henry added. The pasture had plenty of grass, a cool rusty-water pond fed by a mountain stream, and a lean-to for when it rained.

Wong said, "Yeah-yeah . . . for fifty cents a month."

Henry scowled at Wong, but he was thinking he could make that much easy, just by shining two pairs of shoes down on Hotel Street. "Why not," he finally said. He gave Wong the five dollars.

Wong had grinned.

And now Henry knew why.

"Try give it some grass," Sammy said.

Henry looked at him, thinking of saying something like, *He don't want grass, you idiot. Can't you see he lives in a field of grass?* Instead, he said, "What I need is a bucket of oats."

"You got a saddle, or you going ride it bareback?"

"I don't have a saddle."

"How come you bought it, Henry? You not a horse guy."

"Because it was only five dollars, and anyways I like horses."

"Just not this one, yeah?" Sammy said, grinning.

Henry spat, then rubbed his chin. "I'll think of something. Let's go down Hotel Street and shine some shoes. I gotta make some money."

"Yeah, good."

Henry looped up the short piece of soft rope and crammed it into the back pocket of his khaki pants.

When the military guys weren't on their bases or maneuvering in the hills or shipping out to some Pacific island, they spent their free time on Hotel Street in downtown Honolulu. And what they did there was stand in line—for tattoos, food, movies, the laundry, bars, and girls. They stood in line for everything, because there were so many of them. Thousands.

Sometimes Henry and Sammy went down there and made good money. It was easy, since all those army and navy guys were just standing in lines. Sammy joked around with them, made like he was real friendly, made small talk, trying to drum up some business. And Henry shined the shoes, snapping his dirty rag and spitting on the shiny black toes. They even talked with the civilian mainland war workers sometimes, who ran around with loud mouths and flashy silk aloha shirts.

But when Henry and Sammy ran across a serviceman or a war worker who was by himself, they would close up like turtles. If it was a bunch of guys, it was easy. A bunch of guys was nobody. But when it was just one guy, then it was a person. And that was not easy, that was different; a person had a name and opinions they didn't want to hear.

The bottom line was Henry and Sammy didn't really like all those servicemen and war workers. Nobody Henry knew liked them. They hated it when somebody called them "boy," or a "native," or when they heard somebody complaining about being on "this godforsaken rock."

Henry's mother, who worked at the pineapple cannery, said the servicemen weren't so bad, it was the war workers who were the troublemakers—the machinists, maintenance crews, assembly line workers, and clerks. "They got a lot of money they don't know what to do with," she said.

And his father, who was a steelworker at Pearl Harbor, told him, "Downtown you got thirty-five, forty guys for every girl, so right off the bat they not very happy. So what do they do? They get drunk and fight, that's what, and you just stay clear of them, Henry. Stay away from Hotel Street. I better not catch you going near that place."

Henry and Sammy left the horse and headed down toward the bus stop to catch the bus to Hotel Street.

On any one day there were about thirty thousand men crawling around Hotel Street. There was no way in the world Henry's father could ever find him there. Unless he was down there himself. And if he was, how could he explain that to Henry?

As they walked, the road so hot you could smell the tar, an army Jeep with three guys in it passed. Nobody waved to anybody.

Sammy said, "What you going call your horse?"

"Killer."

"No, if you call it that, it will think it *is* a killer, and once it thinks that, you'll never get on it. How about Brownie? Or Bucky, since when you ever get on it, it will prob'ly buck you off." He laughed.

"I like Killer better."

"I had a cousin named Johnny, but everyone called him Pee-Wee. Because he was so small, yeah?"

"And now I'm supposed to ask you what that's got to do with calling my horse Killer, right?"

"Everything, because since we was all calling him Pee-Wee, he started thinking maybe he was too small for play baseball, too small for football, too small for work cannery, too small for—"

"Kay-okay, get to the point."

"He ended up as a bookkeeper."

"What's wrong with that?"

"Shhh. Can you imagine writing numbers in a book all day long? Drive me nuts, man."

"How come you said you *had* a cousin? He's dead, or what?"

"No, he moved. Mainland. Couldn't take it."

"Couldn't take what?"

"The numbers."

"Sheese."

"Here comes the bus."

It was full, of course. Every bus at every stop on every day was always sweaty full. But they squeezed onto it anyway, rode standing up, packing in like Vienna sausages. Mostly local people were on it, but there were also some war workers and a few military guys, who all looked young, some almost as young as Henry and Sammy.

One guy on the bus was crammed up close to Henry. He was snappy clean in his khaki uniform. Army guy, probably from Schofield. Henry liked his hat, tilted to the side like it was. The guy caught Henry looking and dipped his chin, Hello.

Henry turned away.

Later Henry glanced at him again. He guessed the guy was probably about nineteen. He had dark hair, almost black. And blue eyes. Henry hadn't seen that very often, black hair and blue eyes.

"Howdy," the army guy said to Henry. The guy was just trying to be friendly.

Henry didn't know what to do.

"My name's Mike," the guy said.

Sammy, who was standing right behind Henry, let out a small scoffing sound that said, *Can you believe this joker is talking to us?*

Henry looked down at his feet.

They rode for thirty minutes more in silence. Once the driver stopped the bus and got out and smoked a cigarette. The drivers did things like that because they had so many customers they didn't care anymore how they treated them, and everyone waited on the bus, afraid to get off and lose their place. When he was done, the driver got back on and continued on toward Honolulu.

Half the people on the bus got off on Hotel Street, Henry and Sammy among them. And Mike, who went off by himself. Funny he was by himself, Henry thought. Mostly those guys went around in packs.

"He likes you," Sammy whispered.

"Shuddup. You're sick, you know? You need help."

"Yeah, yeah."

They walked around. It was hot, the street sending up as much heat as the sun. Every place you looked was jammed with uniforms, white for navy, khaki for army, everywhere.

"Let's go check out the tattoo shops," Sammy said.

"Which ones? There must be fifty of them."

"All of them got Filipino artists," Sammy said. "You know, sometimes they do five hundred tattoos a day. You know what's the most popular? *Remember Pearl Harbor.*"

"How you know that?"

"I know."

"Shhh. You so full of it, Sammy."

"No. It's true. My uncle told me that."

He was probably right, since Sammy had Filipino blood.

"Hey," Henry said, "how about Savage?"

"What?"

"The horse. Call him Savage."

"Junk," Sammy said. "How 'bout Spats?"

"Spats?"

"He got a white foot."

"But he only has one."

"So?"

"So you gotta call him Spat, then. Not Spats."

Sammy frowned. "Sound like somebody spit something."

"The no-name horse."

Sammy said, "What did Wong call it?"

"The horse."

Sammy shook his head. "I still like Bucky."

A fight broke out in front of a bar. Men yelling and shoving. Henry and Sammy ran over to see. A war worker and a navy guy were going at it, but two navy SPs broke it up before it got any farther. The war worker guy went off looking back and swearing at the navy guy, telling him he better watch his back.

"Look," Henry said.

Sammy turned around.

Mike.

Mike smiled when he saw them and came over, saying, "Not much of a fight, huh?"

Henry still didn't know what to do around Mike, or any service guy who was by himself. He sure didn't want to talk to him. But he did wonder where he was from. Ohio, probably. Or maybe Iowa. They were all from places like that— at least that's what his father told him. "From Ohio to the grave," he'd said. "So sad. They're just kids. Farmers and grocery-store stock boys. Come way out here to fight and die."

But Henry never thought about that. He didn't care where they were from. He just knew he didn't like them. Like the rest of his friends.

"Uh . . . yeah," Henry said. "The SPs broke it up."

"So," Mike said, then said no more.

Sammy turned to walk away.

Henry wanted to go, too, but the guy was just trying to be friendly and, well, he wasn't so bad. Henry grabbed Sammy's arm. "Wait."

Sammy stopped and turned back quickly, like maybe Henry was going to fight the guy.

Henry searched for something to say. Nothing came.

"I hate this street," Mike said. "Nothing's real, you know? Don't it seem that way to you?"

Sammy tugged at Henry's arm, like, *Come on, let's get out of here already. We got shoes to shine.*

"Yeah," Henry said to the army guy. "But it's kind of fun to watch all you guys stand around waiting."

Mike shook his head. "That's what we do, ain't it? Wait. Wait for everything. Wait for a cup of coffee. Wait for a shoeshine. Wait for the war."

Henry hadn't ever thought of that before, wait for the war. Strange.

Sammy turned his back to them.

"What's your name?" the army guy, Mike, asked.

"Henry. And this is Sammy," he added, pointing a thumb back over his shoulder.

Finally Sammy turned around. He nodded, but coldly, like maybe he'd rather spit than talk.

"He's not as bad as he looks," Henry said, grinning.

Mike put out his hand to shake.

Henry hesitated but shook. The guy's grip was strong. That was good.

Sammy shook, too, reluctantly, and Henry prayed to heaven that his father wasn't watching from some secret hole in the wall.

"Where you from?" Henry asked, and Sammy threw his head back as if to say, *Jeez, you gotta be kidding, come on, let's go.*

"Tyler, Texas. Ever heard of it?"

"No. But I heard of Texas."

Mike nodded, then dipped his head toward the rope hanging out of Henry's pocket. "What's the rope for?"

Henry turned to look. He'd forgotten all about it. "Uh . . . oh, that. I got a horse. Me and Sammy was riding it today."

Sammy stifled a laugh.

"No kidding," Mike said. "What kind of horse is it?"

"A brown one."

"A brown one?"

"Yeah, brown."

Mike scratched the back of his head and thought a moment. "You think . . ." He paused, thought some more. "You . . . you think I could ride your horse? I ain't seen mine in six months."

That woke Sammy up. He grinned. "Sure, you can ride it," he said.

Henry said, "He's kind of . . . well, he don't let nobody ride him but me." The last thing he wanted was to have this *haole* messing up his horse. And if his father ever heard of it, he'd—

"Got him trained, huh?" Mike said.

Sammy laughed.

"What?" Mike asked. "You boys pulling my leg?"

"No-no," Henry said. "I really got a horse. It's just . . . hard to ride, that's all."

"Yeah, hard to ride," Sammy added. "We can't even catch it."

Henry thought, *We?*

"Bet he'd let me on him," Mike said.

"How much?" Sammy asked.

"What do you mean?" Mike said.

"You said you bet. How much?"

Mike grinned. "Okay. How much you got?"

That stopped Sammy, who was broke as a lizard. He waved Mike off, as if to say, *Forget it already.*

"Tell you what," Mike said. "If I can't ride the horse, I'll give each of you five bucks. But if I *can* ride him, then you let me visit him once in a while. How's that?"

"You got a deal," Sammy said, sticking out his hand to shake.

"Hey," Henry said. "It's not your horse to bet."

"Sure it is," Sammy said. "I'm the trainer."

Okay, Henry thought. *Fine.* What did he have to lose, anyway? If he got five bucks from Mike, the horse would be free. He shook hands with Mike. "Let's go, then."

Mike grinned. "Now you're talkin'."

The horse was way over on the far side of the field, standing in the blue shade of a mango tree. The air was still, no breeze, no cars or people around. Henry, Sammy, and Mike leaned against the rotting wood fence, batting flies away from their faces, studying the horse.

"He ain't a purebred or anything," Mike said. "But he don't look bad. Nice lines, nice head. He got a name?"

"Bucky."

"Not Bucky," Henry said, shoving Sammy. "He don't have a name yet. I'm still thinking about it."

"How long you had the horse?" Mike asked.

"A week."

Mike nodded. "Let's go take a look."

Mike stepped up and over the fence. Henry and Sammy followed him into the pasture, single file.

On the other side, the horse stood staring at them, head up, ears cocked forward. When they got about halfway across, the horse bolted and trotted down to the lower corner.

Mike stopped and looked around. About two acres of grass and weeds. A few trees. He turned to the pond near the lower end where the horse was now. "How deep is the water?"

Henry shrugged. "I don't know. Five or six feet. In the middle. I don't think it's any deeper than that."

Sammy said, "You got two five buckses on you?"

Mike pulled out a small folded wad of bills, and Sammy's eyes grew into plates. "Don't you worry, I got it. But the thing is, I'm keeping it, because me and that horse down there are going to get along just fine."

Sammy grinned. "That's what you think."

Mike said, "Stay close behind me, and walk slow."

The horse raised its head and trotted off a ways. Mike stopped and the horse stopped, looking back at them. With his eyes still on the horse, Mike reached back, saying, "Let me have that rope."

Henry handed him the rope from his back pocket.

Mike let one end of it drop, then looped it back into his hand. "You boys go stand over by the fence."

Henry and Sammy went down to the fence, walking backward. "What are you going do?" Sammy asked.

"Make friends. Talk a little."

"Talk?" Sammy snickered, then mumbled to Henry, "You heard that? He going to talk to the horse." He half laughed, then glanced back at Mike. "This I gotta see."

"Me too," Henry said. "The guy strange, yeah?"

Mike walked over to the pond. He studied it a moment, then looked up. The horse was on the other side of it now, watching him.

Sammy said, "Pretty soon he going see why we call him Bucky."

Mike walked around the pond.

The horse headed away, not running, just keeping a certain distance with one ear cocked back toward Mike. It snorted once and threw its head.

Mike stopped again. This time he looked to the side, not directly at the horse.

The horse stood waiting.

Mike walked away from it. Just kind of strolled off. And the horse took a few steps toward him. Amazing.

Mike stopped.

The horse stopped.

Mike walked, and the horse followed.

This went on for a few minutes until the horse finally walked all the way up to Mike's back. But Mike didn't try to put the rope over his neck. In fact, he didn't even turn around. He just stood with his back to the horse. When the horse was only a couple of feet away, Mike finally turned and faced it. He said something softly.

"What he's saying?" Sammy asked.

"Who knows. Weird, man."

"You telling me."

Mike reached up to put his hand on the horse's nose. And the horse didn't throw his head like he always did when Henry got near him. Mike said something again, and reached into his pocket.

"What's he got?" Sammy asked.

Henry didn't answer, too interested in how Mike was taming the horse.

The horse ate whatever it was Mike had in his pocket, and Mike ran his hand along its neck. Then, slowly, he looped the rope around the horse's nose, making a kind of rope bridle. There was a name for it, but Henry couldn't remember what it was. *Hack* something. Anyway, the horse let Mike do it, just let him.

"Look at that," Henry whispered.

"He still ain't riding it."

Mike led the horse over to the pond, then let the end of the rope fall to the ground. The horse stood still.

Mike took off his shoes and socks. He took off his hat and set it on the shoes. Then his watch.

"What he going do now?" Sammy said. "Go swimming?"

"Shhh. Quiet."

Mike unbuttoned his shirt, took it off. Then his pants and olive-green undershirt. He looked back at Henry and Sammy and grinned.

"Look at that dingdong, standing there in his boxers."

"I think you're right. He's going swimming."

"Man, that guy is white."

"Look like a squid."

Mike led the horse into the pond, talking to it and easing it in slowly. The horse went willingly. No problem. Right in, up to its chest. Mike dipped his hand in the water and scooped up a handful, then let it fall over the horse's back.

"He's giving it a bath," Sammy said.

Henry frowned. What was the guy *doing*?

Then Mike leaned against the horse. Just leaned.

A minute or two later, he threw himself up over its back, so that he lay over it on his stomach, like a blanket. The horse moved but settled down quickly.

"Ahhh," Henry whispered. "The guy is smart, very, very smart. He going get on him in the water, where the horse can't run, or throw him off, or if he does throw him off, going be an easy fall. Smart."

When the horse was settled, Mike eased up on its back and sat, bareback. For a long moment he just sat.

Henry grinned. He liked what he was seeing. Someone could at least get on the horse, even if it was a mainland army guy. Mike was okay. He didn't call anyone "boy" or "native" or complain about where he was.

Mike took up the rope bridle and nudged the horse with his heels. The horse jumped, then walked out of the pond. Mike rode around the pond. Rode up to the top of the pasture, then back.

Henry thought Mike looked pretty good on him.

Mike clucked his tongue, and the horse broke into an easy run. Mike rode smoothly on its back, and Henry could hardly believe that someone could ride a horse like that with no saddle and not bounce off.

"I don't believe it," Sammy said.

"The guy knows what he's doing."

"Unlike us."

"Yeah, unlike us."

A few minutes later, Mike rode up. Stopped, sat looking down at them. "This is still a fine horse, Henry. He's a little old, and he hasn't been ridden in a while, but he's been ridden in the past."

"He wouldn't even let me near him."

"You just have to know how to talk to him, that's all."

"Stupid to talk to a horse," Sammy said.

"No, it ain't. It's part of gaining his trust. After that, he'll let you ride him."

Sammy frowned.

Henry said, "Well, I guess you won the bet."

"You want to try riding him?"

"Nah."

"Come on. He's your horse."

"It won't let me on it."

"Sure he will." Mike slid off. "Come, stand here by him, let him smell you, let him look at you."

"Uh . . . I don't know," Henry said.

The horse twisted an ear toward him.

"Go ahead," Mike said. "Rub his nose, tell him he's a good horse."

Henry inched closer and rubbed the horse's nose. It was soft, soft as feathers. The eye was big and shiny. Brown. "Nice horse," he said, like you'd say to a dog.

"Good," Mike said. "Here, take the rope. Walk around, let him follow you."

Henry led the horse around the pond.

Mike and Sammy stood silently watching.

Out on the ocean two destroyers and a transport ship were heading away from Pearl Harbor. In the distance you could hear the faint cracking of rifle shots, men maneuvering in the hills. A plane droned by, silver in the clear blue sky.

When Henry got back Mike said, "Okay, see if you can get on him. If he gets jumpy, you can take him into the water like I did. He likes the water. Come up and lean on his side, let him get used to you. Then try to get up on him."

Henry put his arms over the horse's back and leaned on him. The horse's ears turned back, then forward again.

"See?" Mike said. "Now go on, get on him."

Henry took the rope bridle, grabbed a hank of mane, and jumped up on its back. The horse took a few sidesteps, then settled down. Henry grinned.

"See?" Sammy said. "I told you you could ride it if you were nice to it."

Henry rode the horse to the top of the field, then back down again. "He's really *not* a bad horse," he said when he got back.

"No, he sure ain't," Mike said.

Henry rode around the pond two times, then came back and slid off. He took the rope bridle off and set the horse free. But the horse just stood there.

Mike went down to the pond to get his clothes. He was dry now, from the sun. He got dressed and the three of them walked back over to the road.

Mike said, "So it's okay, then, if I come see the horse?"

"Yeah-yeah," Henry said. "Anytime. Just come see 'um, ride 'um, whatever you want."

Mike grinned and shook hands with Henry and Sammy. "Thanks. I hope I can get up here a couple more times before I ship out."

"Yeah, couple times," Henry said. "Hey, what you had in your pocket, that you gave the horse?"

"Jelly beans."

"Hah," Henry said.

"When he does something right, reward him. Always reward good work, good behavior."

Sammy said, "Like when you guys get a medal, yeah?"

Mike looked down and said, "Yeah, like that. Well . . ."

"Yeah," Henry said.

Mike nodded and waited a moment, then nodded again and started down the road to the bus stop.

"He's not a bad guy," Sammy said. "For a *haole* army guy."

"He sure knows horses."

"Yeah."

Henry and Sammy were silent a moment. Henry kept thinking of what Mike had said about waiting for the war. Waiting for the war. He'd never thought of it like that before, all of those guys just waiting to go fight. They'd always just been guys causing trouble around town. But, Henry thought, that was nothing next to the trouble they were waiting for.

"He might die soon, you know, Sammy."

Sammy shook his head. "A lot of them don't come back."

For the first time since the bombing of Pearl Harbor, for the first time since the three-day ship fires and massive clouds of dirty smoke and mass burials, for the first time since the arrest of his Japanese friends and neighbors, for the first time since then, Henry thought about how even now, right now, today, guys like Mike were out there some-where dying in the war, going out on a transport ship and not coming back. Young guys, like him and Sammy. Just kids from Texas.

"I hope he makes it," Henry said.

"Yeah."

"But probably . . ."

In that moment, with those words, Henry changed. He could feel it in his guts, a weird, dark feeling—all those young guys just like him, those guys from the mainland, from farms and towns and cities, coming way out here to wait for the war, to wait, to wait, to wait—then to go. And die. All of them would die, he thought.

Henry winced, then shook his head. He rubbed the back of his neck.

"You know what I going name my horse, Sammy?"

"What."

"Mike."

"Mike?"

"After the guy."

"Yeah," Sammy said. He was quiet a moment, then he said, "Because why?"

"Because that guy . . . he going ship out . . . and he ain't coming back."

"You don't know that."

"One way or the other, Sammy, he ain't coming back."

"What you mean?"

"I mean he going get shot and die. Or he going live through things that going make him feel like he was dead. That's what I think, and it ain't right, you know? It ain't supposed to be that way."

They were both silent for a long while.

Finally Sammy looked back at the horse and said, "Mike."

"Yeah . . . Mike."

The horse took a step forward, grazing. And above the mountains, white clouds slept.

Graham Salisbury

Graham Salisbury grew up in the Hawaiian Islands, where his family has lived since 1820, when his ancestors were missionaries there. Although he was born four years after the bombing of Pearl Harbor, his father was there on that day and survived the surprise attack, but was later killed in action when his Corsair was shot down in the South Pacific. Stories about the war years, Salisbury says, "swirled in my imagination for years." Thoughts about the tragedies of war became even more real for him in the 1960s when one of his schoolmates and surfing buddies was killed in Vietnam after rescuing many others with his helicopter.

World War II provides the background for Salisbury's award-winning *Under the Blood-Red Sun,* a novel about friendship, family relationships, and prejudice in Hawaii in the weeks surrounding the Japanese attack on Pearl Harbor. This novel was not only an American Library Association (ALA) Best Book for Young Adults and an ALA Notable Book, but also a *Booklist* Editors' Choice, an International Reading Association Teacher's Choice, a *Parents' Choice* Honor Award winner, an Oregon Book Award winner, a National Council for the Social Studies–Children's Book Council Notable Trade Book in the Field of Social Studies, and the 1994 winner of the Scott O'Dell Award for Historical Fiction. In 1997 the young people of Hawaii voted *Under the Blood-Red Sun* their favorite book, thereby earning it the Nene Award.

Graham Salisbury's other books—*Blue Skin of the Sea,*

Shark Bait, and *Jungle Dogs,* all featuring teenage boys in
Hawaii—have earned a Bank Street Child Study
Association Children's Book of the Year Award, two more
Parents' Choice Awards, two more Oregon Book Awards, a
School Library Journal Best Book of the Year award, the Judy
Lopez Memorial Award for Children's Literature, and the
1993 PEN/Norma Klein Award.

Mr. Salisbury now lives in Portland, Oregon, and is currently working on two companion novels to *Under the Blood-
Red Sun.* For more details about Graham Salisbury, check
out his Web site at www.grahamsalisbury.com.

1950 - 1959

Many people today view the 1950s as a bland, uneventful period. But the fifties were far from that. First came the Korean War, the spread of Communism, and the increase in Cold War tensions. Exaggerated fears of Communism spawned witch hunts by U.S. Senator Joseph McCarthy against "known Communists" in government and in the film industry. Meanwhile, the Atomic Energy Commission began testing nuclear weapons in the Nevada desert as well as in the South Pacific.

The U.S. Supreme Court, in the case of *Brown v. the Board of Education*, changed the long-held concept of "separate but equal" facilities for minority people, thus outlawing separate rest rooms, separate drinking fountains, and, most importantly, separate schools. Integration, however, was slow to take place, and discrimination against black people continued fiercely in many places in the South. When Rosa Parks was arrested for refusing to give up her seat to a white man on a city bus in Montgomery, Alabama, her act became a symbol for the civil rights movement under the leadership of Reverend Martin Luther King, Jr.

This was also the decade of the first human kidney transplant, the heart pacemaker, the Salk polio vaccine, and the heart-lung machine that made heart surgery possible. There was also the world's first credit card, Holiday Inn, Pizza Hut, diet drink (Metrecal), passenger jet, IBM computer, and Barbie doll. And Bill Haley and the Comets, along with Elvis Presley, brought us rock and roll.

As the development of long-range missiles increased the fear of nuclear attack by the Soviet Union, American schoolchildren were given procedures to follow, and some individuals dug bomb shelters in their backyards. How various people handled their doomsday fears is illustrated in the next story about two teenagers with very different outlooks.

We Loved Lucy

by Trudy Krisher

Every Saturday morning I was startled from sleep. The alarm was a blast from the muzzle of my father's shotgun; it rocketed me from my weekend slumbers.

After breakfast my father dumped the blasted carcasses of rabbits and squirrels onto the kitchen table next to the butter dish and the ketchup bottle.

He struck me then as a puny figure on the world's dangerous stage. He was different from the fathers of the other kids I knew. Those fathers took full-fledged, manly hunting trips to icy lakes and snow-capped ranges. They returned with the grand trophies of antler-headed deer or sharp-toothed grizzlies. My father took aim at critters scurrying through the woods at the back of our house, felling them with gray bullets shaped like missiles and dumping his feeble trophies into my mother's old pillowcases. As I stared into the unblinking rodent eyes that gazed blankly at me beside the salt and pepper shakers, I grew red with shame at the evidence of innocent and random death at the hands of my own father. His hunting exploits seemed a needless cruelty, like swatting a fly with a sledgehammer or felling a spider with an A-bomb blast.

Outside of Saturdays, my father was a quiet man, a man of few words whose grunts and mumbles passed for conversation. He was a newspaper reader, the cover-to-cover kind, and my childhood memories are accompanied by the rattle of newspaper pages, a sound signaling an undercurrent of war, like the clanking of sabers or the clomping of cavalry hooves. It seemed to me as if all the words my father ever needed were ingested from newsprint and swallowed whole. He took them in as a kind of food, and when he did speak, the words were emitted only sparingly, a few at a time, like burps.

My shattered Saturday sleep paralleled a time when my own identity was itself shattered, wavering unsteadily like the pitches of the boys' voices in my seventh-grade classroom. In 1951 a summer had passed since North Korea invaded the South, a historical danger that was as distant and vague to me as the Civil War we had studied in our social studies texts. I imagined the conflict in the Pacific as a kind of War Between the States, with slant-eyed Northern blues attacking yellow-skinned Southern grays. I should have read the seriousness of the news from my father's face, for the Korean conflict absorbed all my father's attention, drawing him even more deeply into his newspapers.

But the only danger I felt that fall as I entered junior high was the threat of change. It was a time of transition for me. At my elementary school, I had been on the top rung of the social ladder; in junior high, I slipped swiftly to the bottom. When I looked up, all I could see was a long, treacherous climb. Nearing the end of sixth grade, I had watched the first-graders at their tame games, like Duck Duck Goose, swelling with sixth-grade pride at the wild and passionate kickball games into which we, the older students, hurled ourselves. We played mightily, hating our opposing team as violently as Americans hated the Russians, staking every ounce of energy on winning at any cost.

In junior high even play was different. My younger years had been a simple romp on teeter-totters and monkey bars, but play was now organized into a physical education class that meant sweating on the waxed floor of a gym, donning a military-blue gym suit, and playing by rules for which there were tests and grades. A new ethic of gamesmanship had sprung up in junior high. Play was no longer a grand release of tension but a petty buildup of it. Play had turned underground in a kind of psychological warfare that involved the taunting of teachers and the mimicking of certain peers. We seventh-graders had acquired a one-upmanship ethic, an us-against-them mentality, no longer outlasting the teachers through sheer physical energy, but outwitting them through psychological trickery. For me, play had lost its fun; it had turned deadly serious.

The larger world in which we lived had become more serious, too. New activities that underscored its dangers invaded even the classroom. We practiced civil defense drills, placing our heads on our desks and covering them with our arms. Mr. Terwilliger, our math teacher, was especially alarmist, running us through duck-and-cover drills that required us to hide under our desks. He insisted that Mr. Wrinkle, our principal, provide us with military-style dog tags so our parents could identify our bodies after a nuclear attack.

Once a month the whole school practiced a full-fledged drill that sent us to the basement, where the aluminum heating ducts looked like giant silver versions of my father's shotgun barrels. The routine was to crouch near a wall and shield our eyes.

That is how I met Brenda Wompers. As I peeked through the cracks of my fingers, Brenda Wompers was crouching next to me.

"Scary, isn't it?" She had bugged out her eyes and flung her spread fingers wide.

I jumped back, startled by her wild gesture. Then I choked back a giggle.

"I guess it's scary," I replied with a shrug. One of the rules of junior high was never to admit what you were really feeling, to mask your emotions under a veneer of indifference.

"Dern right," she said. Then she whispered conspiratorily at me, "And do you know who's the biggest scairdy cat of all?"

I scanned the floor of the basement. My classmates were hunched against the basement walls like soldiers in bunkers. They all looked frightened to me. I shook my head. "I dunno."

"Brad Findlay."

She couldn't have been right about that. Brad Findlay was the biggest boy in our grade. In fact, he was the biggest boy in the whole school. He had broad, hulking shoulders and wore triple-E shoes. The ninth-grade football coach was trying to draft him from the seventh-grade team. "How do you know?" I asked.

"The broken pencils," she said. "After every civil defense drill, Brad Findlay goes back to class with a broken pencil. You watch next time, Nancy. When the siren sounds, Brad Findlay puts his pencil between his teeth on his way to the basement, and by the time the drill is finished, he's clamped down so hard his pencil has snapped in half."

Brenda Wompers ignored my silence and kept on talking in the face of it. "My favorite part's the cities with the circles around them. What's yours?"

I couldn't imagine how Brenda Wompers could call the cities with the circles around them her favorite part. The civil defense officer made a practice of showing us a huge map of the United States. Cities like Seattle and Omaha had big red bull's-eyes ringed around them, as if marked for target practice. The circles made me shudder. The centers of the bull's-eyes were black and shiny, like the eyes of my father's animal victims.

"The circles remind me of Mrs. Yost when she bends over wearing that polka-dot dress of hers." Mrs. Yost was our social studies teacher, as wide as she was tall. Brenda Wompers made a pistol with her fingers. "Blam," she said, blasting an imaginary Mrs. Yost's polka-dotted behind. "Bull's-eye."

I swallowed a giggle. Brenda Wompers kept on talking. Her talking soothed the scary churning in my stomach.

"I like the house pictures, too," she said. Brenda talked in a raspy whisper, like someone who was hoarse with a cold. "They're neat."

I thought back to the house pictures the civil defense

officer brought to school. One series of pictures showed a small house barely a mile from ground zero. When the bomb went off, the house was first scorched, then engulfed in flame, and finally shattered by a shock wave that ripped it to pieces.

"Only takes forty seconds flat to rip that place to shreds!" Brenda elbowed me in the ribs approvingly. "That's faster than it takes Janice Burton to spread a rumor!"

The all-clear sounded, and we rose from our fetal positions. As we started back to class, we clanged our heads on heating ducts as cold and hard as the metal sheaths of missiles pointed at us from the Soviet Union.

I swallowed hard and looked into Brenda's face. Her nose was tilted at a skewed angle, and the right front tooth crossed slightly over the left. Those features told me Brenda Wompers hadn't been fashioned on an assembly line. She was unique.

All of a sudden Brenda raised her arm and gave the hollow heating duct a swift smack. The sound was like two garbage can lids played as cymbals. Startled, all the seventh-graders shrieked, then giggled, and then they went stomping up the stairs back to class roaring with laughter. In spite of the blare of the all-clear alarm that still echoed in my ears, their laughter, like mine, had dissolved their anxiety. Something about Brenda Wompers had made it possible for me to leave my secret fears behind in the basement.

After that basement introduction, Brenda and I became fast friends. She was the only person I knew who admitted what was happening to us that year: the deadly earnestness of play, the psychology of seventh-grade warfare, the fear that masked itself as indifference. As she turned things upside down with her humor, we laughed about the changes in ourselves and others of which no one spoke: the acne that spread like raspberry seeds on our cheeks; the sweat of anxiety, which demanded deodorant; the cotton-ball puffs of girlish nipples, which gave us hope for womanly breasts. Inside, in that tender place near the heart where I hid my secrets as tightly as anyone else, I sensed that Brenda Wompers was someone I could trust.

Brenda's house, I happily discovered, was only a few blocks from mine, and yet it seemed a world away, as different from the culture of my house as the Russians from the Americans. Mrs. Wompers lived in her curlers and house slippers, and Mr. Wompers seemed not to mind her pink quilted robe that bore the gray streaks of ashes from her cigarettes. At our house, my mother curled her hair in secret when my father wasn't around, and she declared that house slippers were to be worn only "*before* nine *a.m.* or *after* nine *p.m.*"

At Brenda's house, the doughnut crumbs lingered for days on the counter. At our house, my mother regarded a crumb as a personal affront, requiring instant attack. At Brenda's house, the newspapers were strewn about like vacationers on beaches, with Mr. Wompers occasionally rolling up a newspaper to swat playfully at Mrs. Wompers as he chased her around the kitchen counter. At our house, the newspaper was folded and put away as soon as it had been read, and if my mother fumbled the folding, neglecting to line up the creased edges in the same direction, my father swatted her with his eyes.

Most different of all was the fact that Brenda's family

owned a TV, and every Monday evening I visited Brenda's
house to watch it. At our house, television sets were to be
feared, for my father believed a television would steal our
minds from reading as surely as the Communists would
steal our institutions from democracy. At the Womperses'
house, on the other hand, the television was an object of
affection. The standoffish coldness of the world at my
house was relieved by the warm embraces of Monday
evening at the home of Brenda Wompers.

Monday evenings began with an early supper of pancakes. Mrs. Wompers scraped the pancakes indifferently
from the electric skillet, lavishing them with streams of
maple syrup as thick as cough medicine. After that, Mr.
and Mrs. Wompers and Brenda and I played Parcheesi at
the rickety card table, and as it approached nine o'clock,
Mr. Wompers made a bowl of popcorn for Brenda and me.
Then Mr. and Mrs. Wompers snuggled together on the
couch, throwing an afghan across their legs, while Brenda
and I settled ourselves on lawn chairs that had been
brought in from the patio to be used as extra furniture in
the winter.

At nine o'clock sharp, Brenda snapped on the television, and we watched the familiar letters ribbon themselves
across the thick heart, spelling out the show's familiar title:
I Love Lucy. For half an hour our stiff hearts melted, laughter spilling across the room like a celebration of streamers.

She may have looked like a scatterbrained housewife,
but Lucy Ricardo was simply a lovable clown. Her bright
orange hair was pulled back tightly from a broad face that
registered emotions with clownlike exaggeration. Happiness
was an extravagant upturned smile, and sadness was that

smile turned on its head like the tragedy and comedy masks that graced the class play programs at school. Slashes of lipstick made Lucy's wide lips even wider. Her owl-like, bulging eyes were ringed by thick fringes of lashes steeped in paint buckets of mascara.

Week after week through that fall and into the next spring, Brenda and I roared as we watched Lucy don a slipcover to disguise herself as a chair, impersonate a seal before a bank of horns, and stomp grapes barefooted in a wine-making vat. Each week Lucy, like the seventh-graders we knew in school, tried out a new trick. We could expect Lucy to do the same kinds of things we did: put soap powder in the school aquarium, serve unwelcome guests an open can of cat food in place of tuna fish. But Lucy's dupe was not Mr. Terwilliger or Mrs. Yost, but her own husband, the Cuban bandleader Ricky Ricardo. Each week, true to form, Lucy's tricks backfired dependably, and she was caught in her acts in the same way that our seventh-grade classmates were caught by Principal Wrinkle.

On Monday nights we laughed with the explosiveness of pop bottles shaken hard before opening. We tittered over the stream of an angry Ricky's Spanish epithets: *jesterday* for "yesterday"; *ever thin* for "everything"; *widdout furderadoo* for "without further ado." We loved the way Ricky blew his stack at Lucy every week: "Are you *crazy!*" he screamed, and we could almost see the smoke of anger billowing out his ears.

Our Monday-night laughter streamed across the living room like an uncorked bottle of champagne. It spilled over in fizzy streams that freshened the air of a world grown noxious with the fumes of fear. On Monday nights, before a bottle of seltzer water and a pie in the face, the threat of Communism and seventh-grade stalemates faded.

The Womperses and I watched *I Love Lucy* together all that fall and across the spring and summer and on into the autumn of eighth grade. We loved Lucy.

So did everybody else in America.

Everybody, that is, except the Shellburnes.

At my house, where I had never asked Brenda to visit, things were different. In November we enjoyed a few unexpected days of summer. Like late-breaking, long-awaited news, the days were a kind of appeasement to winter, and we set up the barbecue again. My father poked the hot dogs and ribs with a pronged fork, and my mother brought bowls of red sauce for painting their seared skin. We ate potato salad as an accompaniment and pretended it was still summer.

And then my father made his announcement.

I knew he'd been studying the news even more intently for the last few days. His head was buried in it all the time; he had stared into the headlines as into an open grave. When I watched him, hope rose in my heart that the headlines would be like those in *I Love Lucy*. Unlike my father, the Lucy whom Brenda and I loved scanned headlines that turned into comic plots: "Bull Escapes Farm"; "Robbers Rumored in Area"; "Tropicana Club Seeks New Dancer." But no laughter rose from the pages of newsprint in my father's hands.

He rose from his chair at the dinner table. I had never seen him rise to speak before. From my sitting position, I could see how tall he was, how skinny. His shadow made the tall, thin profile of a missile silo against the dining

room wallpaper. "We Americans have exploded the first
H-bomb," he announced. "Over the Marshall Islands."

The impact of his news was diluted as I struggled to
identify the Marshall Islands. Were they in the Atlantic or
the Pacific? Were they somewhere near Hawaii? I couldn't
place them in pictures in any of my geography books.

"The bomb wiped out an entire island. It no longer
exists."

I sighed, not certain whether to be happy or sad. There
would be no need for me to identify a Marshall Island on a
geography test now. They would have to strike it from the
geography books.

I stared at the grilled chicken on my plate, admiring
the neat crosshatchings of grill marks that flavored it.

"The heat produced was five times that of the interior
of the sun."

The chicken flesh before me was no longer appetizing;
it seemed, somehow, charred beyond recognition.

"The cloud of radioactive coral dust and water rose
twenty-five miles into the stratosphere and spread a hundred miles across the sky."

A single floweret of cauliflower rested on my dinner
plate. With its broad billowy cloud atop its narrow stalk, it
looked to me like a miniature nuclear cloud.

Now my father sat down. I was waiting for him to give a
giant wink. It was what Lucy always did to defuse danger.
When she had planned some sort of devilish trickery, she
turned her face to the audience, slipping her puckered
mouth to one side of her face and giving a deep, dramatic
wink with her thickly eyelashed eyes. That wink told the
audience that it was all a joke. Ha-ha. She was just kidding.

But my father didn't turn to me or wink. Unlike other fathers, he rarely laughed or even smiled; he was always deadly serious.

Instead, he grabbed a notepad and a pen and began to write. The notepad bore a letterhead that said Acme Insurance Agency. It was the company for which my father worked. I knew that he pushed forms back and forth across his desk all day, an occupation as flat and stale as a room with no windows. What he did for a living was part of my shame of him, for his paychecks resulted from people's fears of dying or falling ill or suffering fires or automobile collisions.

The pen he held sported gold letters that said Ask Me About Acme. For an instant I saw the *m* in *Acme* replaced by an *n,* and I thought of Jesse Pierson, the round boy with the pink-blotched face who sat in my English class. Ask Me About AcNe. I pictured Lucy's sliding mouth and broad wink. *Ha-ha. Just kidding, Jesse.*

My father was writing furiously as he talked. He had picked up some civil defense manuals. One of them lay beside him on the table: *How to Build Your Own Bomb Shelter.* He had decided on double-walled concrete and steel joists. He had decided to begin digging now and then finish the work in the spring. He would start the shelter at the end of the patio.

"The end of the *patio,* George?" my mother shrieked.

My father silenced her with an eyebrow raised like a gun barrel.

I saw her chest fall like my own hope. She and I had both dreamed that the square of grass at the end of the patio would one day be turned into a swimming pool. She desired it for the envy it would arouse in her neighbors and her friends at the women's club. I desired it for the bronze cast it would give to my pale white cheeks and shoulders. I had imagined the cool blue water washing over me. Now the square of grass at the end of the patio would be something I would plunge into when our city became the center of a red-and-black bull's-eye on a civil defense map. It would not be a place where I could be baked a toasty brown; it would now be a place where I could be singed into oblivion.

My father's eyes caught mine. He must have seen something crouching there. Like fear. Like the look in the eyes of the cornered creatures at the end of his gun sight on a Saturday morning.

After that my father spent every night after work digging up the ground beside the patio. He rented a backhoe, bringing it into the garage under the cover of darkness so the neighbors couldn't see what he was doing. If they wondered about George Shellburne and his nightly burrowing, they were likely to think he was digging a foundation for next summer's swimming pool, and when he had poured the first layer of concrete for the walls, they could imagine that his project was moving along right on schedule. But as I watched the first layer of concrete slowly drying, the reality of my father's plan set in. I felt as Lucy must have during that Monday-night episode when she got an urn stuck on her head and couldn't wrest it free.

Once the days predictably froze, our family spent its first nuclear winter. We gathered supplies like squirrels. My father bought an oxygen tank and a three-way portable radio. He bought a pick-and-shovel combination for digging out after the blast. He bought a chemical toilet.

He had jobs for us, too. He encouraged my mother to make a list of canned goods she needed, for he would be installing pantry shelves in the shelter come spring. She made a checklist: potted beef, cereal, powdered milk, sugar. The list included the cans of lima beans I hated and the corn I loved. As she checked the items off the list, my mother sighed. I wondered if she was dreaming of the kitchen pleasures she would miss: the Jell-O molds that would melt or the curly lettuce leaves that would wilt under the blast at ground zero.

My father encouraged me to gather a first-aid kit, and I procured smelling salts, flimsy strips of gauze, and a droppered bottle of red Mercurochrome. I approached my assignment halfheartedly, for I imagined Band-Aids sliding off melting skin in a futile effort at first aid.

My father's spirits were buoyant. "It's like returning to the pioneer days," he said with uncharacteristic good humor. "Ah, yes, Martha. To a simpler time. When the family could all be together in a one-room cabin. Life pared down to its essentials." His snappy voice was like a smart pull on suspenders.

I stared out the window to the open hole in the winter ground. It seemed a concrete coffin. I remembered one of my favorite Monday-night episodes of *I Love Lucy*. Lucy and her friend Ethel tried to return to pioneer days, to the simpler time of which my father spoke. They had decided to bake their own bread, accidentally using thirteen cakes of yeast and producing a giant loaf that grew as out of control as Pinocchio's nose. As the loaf spilled out of the oven and swelled across the room, it reminded me of the mushroom cloud against which my modern pioneer family labored to protect itself. It was, like Lucy's loaf of bread, a Paul Bunyan presence, spreading its inflated malignancy across the face of the planet. The shelter that my father sought for us seemed another of his feeble gestures.

I told no one about my father's project. Not even Brenda Wompers.

Brenda and I had grown even closer. We met between classes at either my locker or hers, whispering about our fellow eighth-graders in English or science class. In the afternoons at Brenda's house, we smeared our lips with lipsticks in shades of coral and hot pink. We used her mother's eyelash curler to press our eyelashes into upswept scallops cemented by mascara. Some days we sneaked cigarettes from the pocket of her mother's pink robe, hiding out in the bathroom and smoking. Between puffs, we rested our cigarettes between the mountainous ceramic breasts that jutted from the chest of the naked lady sprawled across Mr. Wompers's ashtray. Sometimes, while we smoked, I shared with Brenda the poetry I often wrote, and she never laughed at the overwrought images or tearful sentimentality they sometimes displayed.

But I never shared with her the shame I felt over my father and his secret, obsessive work.

Brenda had never been to my house. I had never invited her. Sometimes she expressed curiosity about my family, and I shared descriptions that were safe: my father's passion for newspapers, my mother's obsession with cleanliness. When Brenda asked if she could come over, she accepted my resistance in the same way that she accepted everything else about me. It was a relief to have a friend like Brenda. It was a release to feel somehow safe.

My parents didn't like the Womperses. My father referred to them as the "Womperjawed," and then he winked at my mother. I wasn't sure why the Shellburnes should dislike the Womperses; I only knew that when I spoke of Brenda, my parents' eyes darted nervously across the breakfast table, as if the Womperses were the Russians: people whose movements had to be watched carefully.

At the breakfast table, over my Wheaties, my father plied me with questions.

"Hasn't Mr. Wompers lost a job just recently?"

"He's out of work right now," I said, my cereal crunching against my teeth. Against the silence, the sound seemed as amplified as the noises from the hi-fi we played at Brenda's house. "His company wanted to transfer him to Los Angeles. He didn't want to make Brenda switch schools, so he quit. He says he'll find something else."

My mother pursed her tiny lips. She wasn't eating. During meals, my mother usually just watched us eat. Later on, after we had finished, she stood at the sink and nibbled at whatever we had left on our plates.

"Wasn't that Mrs. Wompers I saw in the grocery store?" she asked. "With a scarf over her curlers?"

I knew my mother's question was a mark of disdain. In her mind, a lady never left home in curlers, either with a scarf or without. I hung my head. I didn't answer.

My father put down his newspaper and looked at me. I felt like Lucy Ricardo. Lucy was always trying to get Ricky's attention, to get him to look up from his newspaper and talk to her. But once she got it, she was usually sorry she had asked for it.

"Aren't you reading more comic books and fewer real books since you've known Brenda?" my father asked.

My mother had likely discovered my stash of comic books and told my father about them. Their slick covers hovered under my bed as thick and forbidden as dust. Last summer Brenda and I had begun our addiction to *Archie and Veronica, Jughead,* and *Spider-Man.* Occasionally we traded each other for a Classic Comic like *Ivanhoe* or *The Last of the Mohicans* to throw our parents off.

I ignored my father's real question with a diversion. "Mrs. Parlett says we can read a comic-book version of something we're studying. As long as we still read the original." Mrs. Parlett was our English teacher. I had just finished reading the comic-book version of *The Fall of the House of Usher* as well as the Edgar Allan Poe original. I liked the comic-book version better.

"That's not what I mean."

I heaped my spoon with Wheaties, stalling for time. I stuffed the cereal in my mouth, knowing full well what my father meant. "My grades are still good, Dad," I protested, chewing between words.

"Don't talk with your mouth full, Nancy," my mother ordered. My father nodded in agreement.

I chewed and swallowed. "I do my homework at Brenda's house every afternoon. My grades have never been better."

My parents eyed each other carefully. They couldn't argue with that. It was the source of some confusion for them. Could their daughter continue to make high marks if her companions were friends like Brenda Wompers?

"Then with such high grades, Nancy, I guess you'll have time to join your mother and me at the civil defense meeting. They're held only once a week for six weeks. On Monday nights."

"Monday nights!" My cereal spoon hit the edge of my bowl. It catapulted drops of milk and flakes of Wheaties across the kitchen table. My mother jumped from her seat, reaching for the dishcloth. "But I'll miss *Lucy!*"

After school, when I told Brenda about the civil defense meetings, her reaction was identical to mine. "But Nancy," she protested, "you'll miss *Lucy!*"

I could feel something wet beginning to fill the corners of my eyes. We had been doing our math homework at the rickety card table where we played Parcheesi.

"I'll miss Ethel and Lucy fighting with Fred and Ricky, Brenda." Nearly every week Lucy and her friend Ethel tried to get Ricky and his friend Fred to go to the ballet or to the theater or to a fancy restaurant. Fred and Ricky always wanted to go to the fights.

Brenda studied my face. I saw the crooked line of her nose and the tip that veered off at an angle.

The tears were making two tiny pools in my eyes. "I'll miss the Parcheesi games."

Brenda's upper lip began to lift. I could see the place where her right front tooth slipped over the left.

The pools were about to spill over. "And your mother's pancakes."

Brenda laughed then, and my tears held their banks. She jumped from her chair and began prancing around the room. "You're doing it wrong, Nancy," she insisted. She placed her hands on her hips and spread her legs wide. "When you really need to cry about something, you do it like this."

I didn't understand, and my face must have said so.

"Watch!" Brenda said. Then she blew out her breath and shook out her fingers, getting ready. She lifted her eyebrows to the top of her forehead and spread her lips as wide as she could. She picked up the edge of her skirt and raised it to her eyes as a handkerchief. Then she began to wail. "Waaaahhhh! Waaaahhhh!" She was crying loud enough to wake the dead.

Then I bit my lip and stifled a giggle. I could feel my tears receding. I saw exactly what Brenda was doing. She had gone into a loud, exaggerated crying fit just as Lucy did on Monday nights when things didn't go her way.

I slammed my math book shut and jumped up to join her. I tried raising my eyebrows to my scalp and spreading my lips the way Brenda had. I picked up the hem of my skirt and pressed it to my eyes. "Waaaahhhh!" I wailed.

"That's it, Nancy!" Brenda shouted, slapping her hands together. "You've got it!"

And then we both burst into laughter.

The civil defense class was held in a bowling alley. The civil defense officer had googly eyes and spit-shined shoes that slipped across the waxed floor. The class itself was held at the last two lanes of the alley, and as the officer droned on about meltdowns and Geiger counters, his words were accompanied by the detonation of bowling balls and the explosion of bowling pins. The clock on the wall behind us marked the minutes after nine o'clock as a kind of dooms-day clock, and I shuddered. My mind wandered across the images I could use in my poetry: fun-house mirrors, melting clocks, vodka-swigging Russian soldiers leaning against missile silos, slant-eyed Koreans in Civil War uniforms, children staring into dinner plates heaped with cauliflower clouds.

As my mother and father and I left the civil defense classes each Monday night, I knew that I had missed the pancakes and Parcheesi and the opening letters ribboning across the television screen, scripting *I Love Lucy*. But I knew that what I missed most about Monday evenings with the Womperses wasn't the food or the games or the entertainment. It was the laughter. *Ha-ha. Just kidding.* I missed that.

Brenda Wompers continued to be the truest friend I had ever known. She had vowed to act out every episode of *Lucy* that I missed, and the Tuesday afternoons following my Monday-evening civil defense classes were filled with laughter.

Brenda imitated Lucy getting stuck on the practice barre in a ballerina tutu, and I laughed. Mimicking Lucy, Brenda taped her mouth shut to keep herself from spreading gossip, and I laughed. She chased pieces of chocolate down a production line in a candy factory, and I laughed. She tried to keep Ricky from going bald by applying vibrators, mustard plasters, and a plunger to the thinning hair on his scalp, and I laughed. She vowed to make their apartment more like her husband's native Cuba, bringing chickens, palm trees, and a mule to their home, and I laughed. The laughter was fresh and free, like air cleaned of radioactive fallout.

The civil defense classes had inspired my father. All spring, while the ground thawed, he worked like a beaver on the shelter. On a cool May afternoon, as beautiful as any day I had ever spent on the planet, he put down his tools. The shelter was finally finished.

He invited us into our nuclear bunker to share in his pride. He had put up the shelves for my mother, and her canned goods were lined up like targets in a shooting gallery. He had built bunks along one wall, and my mother had made them up neatly with blankets and sheets. I shuddered, imagining how well I would sleep with the world above the shelter bursting into flames. My father had added a stash of incandescent bulbs, fuses, and a nonelectric clock that ticked loudly next to my mother's food supply. In the corner was a Sterno stove and a jug of water, ten gallons' worth, exactly as the civil defense instructor had recommended. My mother had even added wallpaper to one wall of the shelter, a perky blue-and-yellow flower pattern that added a touch of false cheer to our ominous surroundings.

My father sighed with satisfaction. "We've done a right nice job, Martha, don't you think?"

My mother nodded, her brown curls bobbing up and down.

"Did we leave anything out?"

She wrinkled her nose, thinking. "I don't think so, George."

"Well, Martha," he said, "I think you and Nancy ought to be able to pick out something to bring with you. Something you'd hate to leave behind."

I wondered what he could be talking about. I was certain my father was mad. If the whole world dissolved above me, what could I possibly bring along for comfort?

My mother nodded again. "I'd like to bring the good silver, George." My mother's good silver was brought out on important occasions. I had trouble imagining myself at a meal in the bunker, eating potted meat and canned peas with a silver fork. "And maybe my curlers, George. I wouldn't be able to get my hair done. I'd need my curlers."

He looked down at her paternally, as if she were a bunny or a newly hatched chick in need of his manly protection.

"What about you, Nancy? What would you want to bring?"

He gave me the same paternal look; I was filled with disgust.

I looked him in the eye and said, "Brenda Wompers. I'd like to bring Brenda Wompers with me."

Images of my friend floated into my mind: the crooked teeth and the skewed nose and the upper lip poised to lift into laughter. I thought about the uncorked fizz of laughter on Monday nights at Brenda's house and the popcorn that sprayed from the bowl in a white-kerneled fountain when we laughed too hard. I knew I had made the right choice. If there was anything I had to take with me, it would be Brenda Wompers. Brenda Wompers and her laughter.

My mother and father looked at each other the way they did over the breakfast table when I said I wanted to wear lipstick to school or stay overnight at Brenda's house.

My father said nothing. He simply picked up his shotgun from its place in the corner. He ran his hand lovingly up and down the barrel.

He held it to his eye and peered through the sight. "They say the first blast'll be the bomb itself."

Then he put the barrel down and looked at me. "The second blast, they say, will be the sound of folks shooting their neighbors."

I felt caught in a rifle sight. What was he talking about? I pictured our shelterless neighbors running about, panicked by the nuclear blast. They scampered frantically like the squirrels and rodents my father took aim at on Saturday mornings. They would be terrified, searching desperately for loved ones, seeking shelter from the nuclear tornado, frantically running about like Dorothy in Kansas.

What if the neighbors my father willingly shot included a child? What if it was Patsy Early, just learning to ride a tricycle? *Blam!* What if it was Mr. Borchers, who leaned over his rake for a long chat every fall? Or Miss Simmons, who gave out Baby Ruths *and* Butterfingers on Halloween? *Blam!* Or Brenda Wompers? What if the someone my father aimed to shoot was my best friend?

My father set his rifle in the corner. He turned his back to me. He moved to the shelf and began to mumble, "God helps those who help themselves." He began rearranging the cans on the shelf.

His back was to me. I wanted to scream. I wanted him to turn to me, to let his mouth slide to one side of his face, to stretch his lips downward, to let one eye give a big, broad, dramatic wink. Like Lucy. Ha-ha. I wanted him to say that he was just kidding. *Ha-ha. I was only kidding, Nancy.*

My mind raced with questions as I watched my father stack the cans. What about what God had said about loving your neighbor? Would a faithful Christian in good conscience ever build a bomb shelter? I watched as first my father lined up the cans in one long, straight line. Then he took half the cans and stacked them on top of the other half. Would the fallout of nuclear war include killing your neighbor? What would be the point of life if you had to become a savage to survive?

I could feel the tears welling in the corners of my eyes as I watched my father. He had decided to make pyramids of the cans. He had set one can atop a base of two. I could feel my eyebrows lift to the top of my forehead. I could feel my lips spreading wide. I wanted to reach for the corner of my skirt and hold it to my eyes. *Waaaahhhh!* I wanted to wail. *Waaaahhhh!*

And then finally, in a kind of thermonuclear instant, my secret, my shameful secret, was out.

It happened innocently enough. I had left my math book at Brenda's house one afternoon, and she brought it over that night, knocking quietly on the door after we had finished supper.

We hadn't heard her at first. My mother and I were out back by the patio, inspecting the shelter, while my father was in the bedroom, assembling his latest purchase for us.

I jumped when I saw Brenda behind me. I felt spooked.

"Sorry, Nancy," she said. "Maybe I shouldn't have come in. I—I knocked, but I guess you didn't hear me. The door was open, so I hope this is all right."

My mother rushed up, inspecting my friend the way she looked over meat in the butcher's case. "That's all right, dear. We can't hear the door when we're in the back."

"Here's your math book, Nancy. You left it on the card table. I thought you might need it tomorrow."

"Thanks," I said.

It was then that my father appeared. He was unrecognizable even to me at first. His body was covered in clear plastic, the kind my mother laid over the hall carpet so that it wouldn't pick up stains. The plastic gave a cold crunch as he walked. His head was hooded in a helmet with a visor that slipped down over his eyes. On his back was a tank that looked like something a scuba diver wore when he dove down deep into the ocean.

"It's the fallout suit I ordered," he said. "It came in the mail today." I couldn't see his mouth moving because of the visor, but I could hear the muffled glee in his voice. "Only twenty-one ninety-five."

My mother stepped up to him, patting his plastic arm. "Nancy's friend Brenda is here, George," she said, gesturing in Brenda's direction. "She came to return Nancy's math book. Wasn't that nice?"

My father removed the helmet from his head. Sweat beads lined up along his forehead. He frowned deeply. He eyed my friend suspiciously, as if she were a Communist. "Why didn't you call first?" he said.

Awkwardly Brenda stumbled out the door.

I didn't sleep at all that night. I tossed wildly, thrashing against the sheets. Finally I got up and dressed for school while the dark night surrounded me. I reached for my journal and began to write. I scribbled out images of huge men in space suits floating in black voids of space, of red-haired women with bulging eyes crying tears the size of windowpanes and reaching for hankies the size of tablecloths to dab at their eyes. Worst of all, I imagined the limp body of Brenda Wompers draped across our kitchen table, her tiny blank eyes staring up at me, the paper-napkin holder next to her chin. Finally I fell asleep over my own words.

I tried to avoid Brenda at school that day. She wouldn't let me. She met up with me at my locker. "It's okay, Nancy," she said. "I know you're embarrassed. I still want you to come over after school. I've got something to show you."

I was uneasy as I moved up the walk in front of Brenda's house, my social studies book under my arm. I tried to take comfort in the familiar things I saw there: the ceramic deer bent to nibble on the dry lawn, the limp stalks of thirsty flowers, the spare tire and jack Mr. Wompers had left out in the driveway for weeks.

When I knocked on the door, Brenda threw open the door to greet me. I was astonished by what I saw.

I could hardly tell it was Brenda. She had draped herself in waxed paper held together with masking tape. The waxed paper covered her torso, arms, and legs. She must have unrolled the entire blue box of Cut-Rite that her mother used to wrap Brenda's sandwiches. On top of the waxed paper Brenda was wearing a wide aluminum-foil collar and cuffs. A rubber hose, pulled from her mother's vacuum cleaner, stretched from her waist to the black backpack that hung across her back. She had an empty fishbowl on her head, so her features looked distorted through the wavy glass. Through the glass I could hear her making crackling Geiger-counter noises in her throat; it was the same noise we used to make the sound of creaking doors when we told ghost stories.

"Nancy," she said, speaking as if in slow motion, as if she were shouting through water, "why didn't you call first?"

I could feel the laughter rising from deep inside me somewhere. It came slowly at first, like a punch line I hadn't quite figured out. The laughter started somewhere below my belly button and then gathered power quickly. It rose like carbonation to my throat and then across my teeth and out my mouth. As I threw my arms around Brenda, crushing the waxed paper, wrinkling the collar of aluminum foil, my head bumped against the glass fishbowl, and she grinned, lifting it from her head.

The laughter kept coming. It tumbled from us swiftly like red carpet rolled out for a wedding. I watched Brenda's head emerge from the fishbowl, and in a bright flash all the terrifying images evaporated: the staring rodent eyes and the seared flesh and my father's shadow like a missile silo against the wall. She turned her profile to me, slipping her red-lipsticked mouth to one side of her face and giving a deep, dramatic wink with her thickly eyelashed eyes. That wink, as swift and bright as any nuclear flash, was my defense. Against the cold war that raged within. Against the cold war that raged without. *It was all a joke, Nancy,* that wink said. *Play along with me. Ha-ha. Just kidding.*

Trudy Krisher

Born in Macon, Georgia, Trudy Krisher grew up during the 1950s in south Florida. The fifties, she says, "provide a rich source of information about our culture that is relevant to today: American notions of success, of family, of national destiny." Although she, like many others at that time, was anxious about the possibility of nuclear war, her own family never built a bomb shelter. Her father, she says, "never lifted a hammer or raised his voice."

As a teenager growing up in the South, Krisher noticed the disparity between the ideal of equality proclaimed by American society and the reality of racial discrimination that occurred around her. Those concerns eventually led her to write *Spite Fences,* a novel that looks at racism in a small town in Georgia through the eyes of Maggie Pugh, a poor white teenager, as civil rights sit-ins were beginning. That powerful novel won the International Reading Association's Children's Book Award in 1995 and was a *Parents' Choice* Honor Book and an American Library Association (ALA) Best Book for Young Adults.

Kinship, set in a trailer park in 1961, continues the story of Pert Wilson, a character from *Spite Fences,* as she learns to appreciate the rich and empowering source of love that her tattered community provides. *Kinship* was an ALA Best Book for Young Adults, a Bank Street College Best Book of the Year, and a New York Public Library Book for the Teen Age in 1997.

Trudy Krisher lives with her three children in Dayton, Ohio, where she is assistant director of the Learning Assistance Center at the University of Dayton. There she teaches developmental writing classes and supervises the campus writing center, the Write Place. At home she is working on a historical novel about a young girl's involvement in the women's rights movement between 1832 and 1848.

1960 - 1969

The "Swinging Sixties" were characterized by long hair, go-go boots, miniskirts, bell-bottom pants, psychedelic art, and sex, drugs, and rock and roll, led by such groups as the Beatles, the Rolling Stones, and the Supremes. "Flower children" wearing peace symbols bloomed in communes across the United States as well as in Europe.

More significantly, the struggle for racial equality begun in the late fifties continued with demonstrations, voter registration drives, race riots, the murders of civil rights activists as well as innocent children, and a march through Washington, D.C., highlighted by Martin Luther King, Jr.'s "I have a dream" speech and the singing of "We Shall Overcome."

Before the decade was over, Reverend King had been assassinated, as had been Black Muslim leader Malcolm X, President John F. Kennedy, and his brother Bobby Kennedy.

Meanwhile, the race between the Soviets and the Americans for dominance in outer space continued, culminating on July 21, 1969, when U.S. astronauts Neil Armstrong and Edwin "Buzz" Aldrin stepped onto the surface of the moon.

At the same time, fighting escalated in Vietnam, with the horrors of war brought into everyone's homes on the television news each evening. As American casualties mounted, so did the protests against the war. "Make love, not war" became the slogan of the times, and people everywhere sang John Lennon's "Give Peace a Chance."

While these momentous events were taking place throughout the world, young people in big cities and small towns were questioning traditional roles and challenging the dictates of the "Establishment." Sometimes the struggle was over something as simple as the length of one's hair, as Benny Woods discovers in this story by Chris Crutcher.

Fourth and Too Long

by Chris Crutcher

I guide my 1938 Chevy pickup across the rickety one-lane bridge, away from the cabin and toward Coyote Creek. Grandma sits beside me, gazing first out the windshield, then out the passenger-side window, seemingly passing through country for the first time that she has passed through most every day for the past seventy-eight years.

"It's hair, Grandma," I tell her. "It's not about drinking or smoking or staying out after curfew. It's protein." I reach across the seat and brush a few strands of her own, white as fishing leader, from her eyes. "Did you know it was protein, Grandma? I'll bet not."

She stares at me blankly, then fixes her gaze on the pot-holed road ahead, which is what I'd better do if I don't want to shake the wheels off this tin can of a truck.

"How far will they take this? Are they willing to throw away the season? Joe Namath has hair all the way down the back of his neck, for crying out loud, and it doesn't affect his game."

Grandma clears her throat and rocks herself slowly in the seat, never the consummate football fan.

"I know, I'm not Joe Namath, but I'm the closest thing to it Coyote Creek has seen."

We drive past the city limits sign: Coyote Creek, Pop. 706. "We'll be into the seventies before this town limps into the sixties. I don't understand it; we get the newspaper, we have TV."

Grandma's head lolls side to side with the music from Patsy Cline singing "Sweet Dreams" on the only AM station we receive because of our position at the vertex between mountains that jut like mammoth skyscrapers.

It's not unusual that I'm getting no response from my grandmother. She hasn't known who I am one day out of five for the past year and a half. A lot of townsfolk say I should have put her in a retirement home after my folks died, but she wouldn't recognize the caretakers there any better than she does me, and I like to think that when she lies down on the same bed she slept in when she was a little girl, at least her *body* knows she's where she belongs. Plus as long as I'm living with her, or vice versa, I'm with an adult relative and don't have to sweat county welfare trying to place me with "responsible" adults. That was a bigger worry just after my folks died. In just more than a week, I'll turn eighteen.

It isn't easy losing your parents, but at least mine were old. They died within two days of each other with heart disease: my father from a heart attack, my mother from a broken heart. They'd been together so long Mom said she couldn't tell where Dad left off and she began, like they melted into each other somehow over that time. It would be nice to say they had a fairy-tale marriage, dancing at the American Legion Hall on Saturday nights, whispering sweet nothings and snuggling up, but to tell you the truth I haven't a clue what they were like together when they were young. They hold the county record for delayed conception, I can say that. I was ten years old on their fortieth wedding anniversary. The kid they should have had when they were twenty-five popped out when they were fifty-one. I'm surprised Dad didn't have his coronary surprise the day he heard the joyous news of my impending arrival, since he'd been told thirty years earlier he had the sperm count of a woman.

So essentially my parents were done raising kids before they had any, which was to my advantage because they let me raise myself. I was more than up to the task; I had done the math and didn't really expect them to outlast my high-school years. To ease my worry, Dad kept pointing out Grandma's age and said that genetically I had nothing to worry about.

I said, "Dad, Grandma puts gravy on her ice cream."

"She gets a little confused, Benny."

"She also gets bad ice cream. How do you know that won't happen to you?"

"I don't like ice cream."

"Neither does Grandma. She thinks it's mashed pota-toes."

"I don't like potatoes, either."

I was never in trouble at home for transgressions at school because, though Dad had an IQ that was out of sight, he'd hated every teacher he had through sixth grade, when he dropped out for good, and neither of my parents had the energy or inclination to get after me, so with every phone call or note from school, my parents would call back and say, "We'll take care of it," and then Dad would shake his head and say, "I ain't dealin' with those assholes, son. If they throw you out, you're on your own."

Most of my trouble in school comes from taking on authority. Since there never was much of it at home, I don't seem to have a lot of respect for it; or at least it doesn't intimidate me like it does other kids. Don't get me wrong— I'm not looking for trouble. I'm looking for a way out.

Anyway, three days after Christmas vacation my sophomore year, I came home and found my mother on the living room floor, Dad's head cradled in her lap, him deader than a brick. They'd been in that position nearly two hours, so resuscitation was out of the question. Mom looked up at me absently and stroked his hair, so I sat with her awhile, then called Dr. Patterson, who came out in his nearly new 1966 makeshift Ford station wagon/ambulance and took Dad away.

That night Mom asked if I'd be okay by myself, and though I knew what she was getting at, I asked where she thought she was going. She said, "With him." I don't know if I was in shock or just naturally detached, but I said if she was going to be with him for eternity anyway, why didn't she take a couple years' break and hang out with me? The morning of Dad's funeral I went to get her from her room, and she was exactly where she'd said she would be.

My parents had zero insurance, had made no arrangements for anything that might happen the day after they were history. We'd lived in a small three-bedroom rental just off Main Street, owned by Mr. Miles, the banker, which meant I could go to work or move Grandma and me out to the broken-down two-room cabin she grew up in—in which neither room was a bathroom. In the dead of a winter night when I hustle those five giant steps across the snow only to press my bare butt next to that twenty-degree-below wood, I believe I should have applied at the sawmill where Dad worked all his life, but during balmier nights I know it's smart to finish high school and give myself a future that doesn't include a shot to the chest from a two-by-four coming off the green-chain at the speed of a small truck.

Right now that future might be in jeopardy over hair; or maybe it's over freedom.

If I were to choose the three things that best describe me, I would say these: I'm a hell of an athlete, I'm pretty darn smart, and I'm uglier than a stick.

I don't mean to brag, but we went undefeated with one tie in football last year, and I was the reason. I wouldn't say that aloud, because my parents did teach me to be humble (actually they taught me to *act* humble). We play eight-man football in Coyote Creek because the high-school population is barely over a hundred, which means even with most guys going both ways, it's hard to scrape up enough players for an eleven-man team. If you don't show up for the first day of practice your freshman year, we come and get you; your choice is to get beat up with pads or get beat up without pads. You could be missing critical body parts and still letter your last two years in Coyote Creek. Some schools in the league are even smaller.

Trouble is, it's almost impossible for a player on an eight-man team to get a college scholarship because most college coaches don't consider it football. But several NAIA schools have shown interest in me based on last year's performance and say if this year is as good or better, they're willing to cover room, board, books, and tuition. I've worked at odd jobs since my parents croaked, but I haven't saved much because Mrs. McMurty, the woman who watches Grandma when I'm in school and playing sports, isn't available for much more time than that. I do get a Social Security check because of my parents' deaths, but Grandma and I eat that up pretty quick. It's *cold* in the winter, which means extra blankets and clothing for her, and I can't stand to see her in secondhand or charity stuff, so I order out of the catalog she used back when she could tell a coat from a bran muffin. Plus I work out *hard*, which means I, alone, have the food bill of a family of three. If I'm going to college next year, it will be because someone is willing to pay me to play ball.

I suppose the other possibility for my higher education could have been an academic scholarship. I do seem to have inherited my father's intelligence when it comes to certain subjects. My grades are off the charts in any subject in which I'm interested; which means English, because I like to write, and American government and current events, because those are the places I can find out why things are getting as crazy as they are in this country, which any graduating senior ought to know, because if your next move is a bad one, you end up in the jungles of a bad place doing bad things. Math and science present different dilemmas altogether, which is why if I'm going to get a scholarship, it will be an athletic one. I am selectively intelligent.

I'm not, however, selectively ugly. My mother used to call my looks "unfortunate." That's like saying Muhammad Ali likes to kid around in the gym. When I was three the neighbor's Doberman took offense at my whacking him across the snout with a plastic shovel and bit off the top of one ear and mangled the other one until it looked like a piece of chewed bubble gum. I guess my parents thought it didn't matter how my ears looked as long as they worked, because nothing was done to repair them and I've got some seriously gnarled ears, which don't make my broken-beak nose, thick lips, gapped teeth, and hooded eyes look one bit better. I look like God got pissed.

Which brings us to the current dilemma about hair.

My coach says either mine is gone by the first day of practice or I don't play, period. He is backed by Mr. Krebsbaugh, our principal. According to this brain trust, the hippie commie pinko bullshit that has been going on in the country is not going to get a foothold in Coyote Creek. Good grooming shows respect, on and off the field of athletics. It is about discipline, they say; about respect. It is about surrendering your personal wants and needs for the good of the many.

Here's my problem with that. When I was in grade school, good grooming meant no jeans and no T-shirts, the only clothes I owned. Dad had been laid off down at the sawmill and we were living on unemployment. The school wouldn't relax the dress code for me, and to accommodate my needs, and those of a few others, they had a clothing drive. For almost two years I had to wear other kids' clothes to school with my gnarled ears. From then on, good grooming has had nothing to do with respect.

I'm not sure what I think of the commie pinko bullshit part of all this, but the hippie part intrigues me. I'm not interested in smoking grass or living in a commune or sharing my girlfriend, if I had one, like they do in California, but I've been drawn to this movement since I was in junior high because if the hairstyle reaches the mainstream (and into the far-reaching tributaries), then I could usher in the era of the unshorn athlete and *cover up these ridiculous ears*! Hell, the main reason my favorite sport is football is that I get to wear a helmet. Only I can't say that—I mean, how would it sound? My dad told me all my life that if I just acted as if my ears were normal, it wouldn't bother me, but that was a lie, because I've pretended they were just like everyone else's forever, and there hasn't been a minute of my life that I wasn't aware of them. But I can't start complaining now, so I have to stick to a more philosophical argument, which is where the intelligence comes in.

To my disadvantage, the dress code has been in effect as long as I've been in school: no jeans or T-shirts—as I said—and no tennis shoes, not even Chuck Taylor Converse All-Stars. Let your hair grow over your ears or long enough to touch your collar and you may not set foot on any playing field or in any athletic arena. "A good Wolverine is a well-groomed Wolverine," they say. I tell them, in the wild a good wolverine is naked.

The lines are drawn. They say I can't play without a haircut, and I tell them, based on what I have gleaned from my American government class, they haven't a legal right to stand on as long as I follow their rules of conduct. They tell me one of their rules of conduct is a dress code, and I reply that I always come to school dressed, and that's not conduct, that's appearance. They say, "You're a funny boy, Benny Woods, but it is our job to help socialize you—difficult as that task may be—before allowing you into the world," and I tell them there's no "allowing" about it, I'm going there as a function of aging, and besides, they need to take a better look at that world, because it's passing them by. They say that world has been going to hell for the past few years and they intend to graduate young men and women who will bring it back. I tell them running a high school of a hundred students in a remote part of Idaho isn't a very good vantage point from which to do that. That pushes the stakes up far enough for them to point out that I have always been impudent and it's too bad I wasn't raised better and if I don't have the hair off my shoulders by first practice, I can kiss my season, and subsequently my scholarship, goodbye.

Often as not, the quarterback of the football team is a good-looking guy who goes out with the prettiest cheerleader and tells funny jokes and is just too cool for words. Probably because of the way I look, I'm way more comfortable with a book than I am with people, and I haven't had a date since the time in junior high I asked Martha Shannon to a hayride and she said she'd like to but her friends would make fun of her. At least she was honest. I got even with her by standing next to her in that year's class picture, looking like I was about to kiss her.

I'm sitting on the porch watching Grandma rock slowly, eyes closed and the hint of a smile on her lips. The afternoon sun is sinking below the high peaks behind the cabin while I debate whether to put on my cleats and run a few wind sprints, maybe fire some balls through the raggedy pickup tire hanging on a rope from a branch of a large cottonwood in the backyard. No athlete goes into the season more prepared than I. Ralph Emerson and I worked out every day this summer, because we know we could win it all this year. I have to think Coach is bluffing about not letting me suit up. Of course, he may be thinking the same about me. Why can't they see what I've always gone through to pretend I don't care how I look? I can assure them no one in school is going to try to emulate my look. Why do they have to make me beg?

I see the cloud of dust first, rolling above the shrubs around the last curve leading to the cabin, then hear the screech of Ralph's fan belt and the rattle of a "body by Fisher" that hasn't been tightened down since his junker of a '57 Plymouth Savoy rolled off the assembly line eleven years ago. That car is a moving traffic citation even without Ralph Emerson at the wheel. In Idaho, you can get a "daylight only" driver's license when you're fourteen, and in our county they administer the driving test by placing a small mirror beneath your nostrils. If the mirror steams up, you drive. Hence Ralph Emerson behind the wheel of a motorized vehicle.

Ralph bails out while it's still lurching, resplendent in Coyote Creek Wolverine shorts pulled over purple sweatpants and a cut-off green sweatshirt that was likely not green when one of his older brothers bequeathed it to him. Ralph tends to ignore the rudiments of personal hygiene sometimes and can get seriously fungal.

"Aw, man," he says when he sees me.

"What's the matter?"

"Your hair!" The word is out. Coach is relying on peer pressure.

"Yeah," I say. "Can't do a thing with it."

He says, "Cut it."

"You're not jumpin' ship on me, are you, buddy?"

Off the field, Ralph is pretty much my only friend. He gets through school on "social promotions" because he isn't even close to sharp enough to do the work, but he's a hell of an athlete and he never gets in trouble, and he does what he's told. He's great to hang out with in the off season because he never complains, and to put it in a crass way, he's so dumb he doesn't know I'm ugly.

"Don' wanna jump on no ship," he says, "but what happens when Coach don' let you play?"

"I'll have more time to do my homework."

Ralphie stands dejected. A tear wells up.

"Hey, c'mon, man, I'm not leaving town. We'll be buddies whether I'm playing or not."

"Yeah, but Rich Dryden's mean. Like, you know, what happens if I go the wrong way again? He don't help me in the huddle like you. Gets Coach hatin' me."

I laugh. Rich is the second-string quarterback, and he's less patient than I am. "Coach doesn't hate you; he just gets pissed when you're the leading rusher for the other team."

"It ain't like it's a touchdown for 'em. An' I only done it twice."

"And not once since the middle of last year," I say. "You're on a five-game streak."

Ralph knows I'm messing with him. "It was foggy."

Coach *was* pissed, especially after the second time. Most leagues have one story in their history of some guy heading north when he was supposed to go south, but Ralph holds the record because *nobody* who ever suffered the humiliation of doing that once could do it again without impaling himself on the goalpost at the end.

In his defense, it *was* foggy, and the field was slippery and muddy and he was cutting back all over the place looking for a hole, but *damn*. If Ralph's IQ were half his belt size, he'd be a scholarship athlete, too, because he can flat *move*, and it takes a couple of guys who really want to, to bring him down. I'm probably the only guy on our team who could have caught him, but I had handed off the ball and faked the rollout, so I was on the other side of the field. Plus I'm not even close to as fast as he is when I'm laughing that hard.

This fight with Coach and Mr. Krebsbaugh over the length of my hair can't really be just about hair. The founding fathers wore wigs to make it look like they had *more* hair. Jesus, whose name Coach and Mr. Krebsbaugh call on all the time, had hair to the middle of his back. Samson was a weenie without hair. Most of the gods in Greek mythology, Prince Valiant, and Sitting Bull; hell, look at Albert Einstein. What about the entire state of California, for that matter? Naw, this is about control.

The sixties are going to be famous someday, I'll bet; like the twenties for "roaring" and the thirties for the Depression and the forties for World War II. I don't remember studying a time in U.S. history that contained more conflict between young and old. Some of it has to do with young people expressing themselves with rock-and-roll music and the way we dress, but I think more has to do with the war in Vietnam and the fact that a lot of guys don't see it the same way as the older guys in town see World War II.

When I was in eighth grade, a kid from our town named Bobby Waters graduated from high school, got his draft notice, decided to join the marines instead, and went to Vietnam. Just like now, a lot of guys enrolled in college or got married quick and had a kid—not necessarily in that order—or dragged up fake medical records for proof of asthma or eczema or bad knees or flat feet, or a hankerin' for other guys. Most of them didn't know where Vietnam was or what we were fighting for and didn't want to take a chance on losing body parts or their lives for something they didn't understand. And yeah, probably a lot of them were scared.

But Bobby Waters wanted nothing to do with any of that. He could have gotten into any college, since he had the grades and the resources, no sweat; but his dad had been a World War II fighter pilot, his uncle a marine who hit the beaches of Normandy the day after D Day. There was tradition. On a leave just days before he shipped out, the town held a rally for him up at the high-school gym. Bobby wore his dress blues that night, looked fit and athletic, with barely enough hair to say he had any. He told us he had an obligation to fight for his country, that every man needed to ante up his part of the price of freedom. He said he didn't have any respect for the hippies and radicals who hid behind their philosophies to mask their cowardice. He said he would make us proud.

Eight months later he came home missing his right leg below the knee, with shrapnel scars dotting his face, arms, and chest like measles. His parents drove him home from the Boise airport in the dead of night, and for nearly a year no one saw more than a glimpse of him or heard his voice. His folks said he was having a tough time readjusting but that they thought it would pass in time. I am one of the few people who actually encountered him. It was a warm summer night, maybe eight months after my parents died. Grandma and I had moved back to the cabin and I was sitting in the outhouse, thinking I should take more dumps at other people's houses so this thing wouldn't fill up before I got out of high school, when I heard crackling in the brush outside. We get plenty of wild game, so I wasn't worried, but when I opened the door to look—with my pants still around my knees—I stood face-to-face with Bobby Waters. Only I didn't recognize him. He looked like Jesus on drugs in a T-shirt and jeans. I froze.

He said, "Hello."

I said hello back and quickly pulled up my pants.

"You know me?"

I shook my head. He could have given me a guess for each person in Coyote Creek, and I'd still have missed it.

He put out his hand. "I'm Bob Waters."

I looked closer, saw no resemblance. "I thought . . ."

"You're Benny Woods."

I nodded again.

"I'm gonna tell you something, Benny Woods."

My heart pounded; this man looked fierce, and twice his true age, if he was really Bobby Waters.

"Don't ever do nothin' nobody tells you without checking it out first."

"What do you mean?"

"You heard me." He pointed behind me. "Mind if I use this? I seen it from the top of the hill. Don't think I can make it home."

I said, "Sure."

He went inside and the door slammed. "Don't forget what I said," the outhouse said to me.

I wanted to talk more, but it seemed in bad taste to stand in the near dark and wait for Jesus from a parallel universe to drop a load, so I left the kitchen door open far enough to see through the screen. Bobby came out and limped back toward the woods, moving pretty well on his prosthesis, and it occurred to me that he might have been wandering those woods at night for some time.

I don't know what happened to Bobby. His parents stopped promising that he would resurface. Some folks say he killed himself. I was going to stop by his folks' house and tell them what he said that night, but I just never got around to it. I think of him sometimes, first standing on the stage in the gymnasium, clean-shaven and shorn, talking brashly and bravely from a point of ignorance, then standing in front of my outhouse, hairy as some abominable snowman, speaking to me from a place of painful wisdom.

So I'm taking Bobby Waters' advice: not doing what I'm told just because I'm told, or because the people doing the telling are older than I am. I don't know Bobby's true story, but in my imagination I see him saying no to the war, going to college, getting married and having kids, and avoiding whatever it was that took his leg and put that look in his eye.

Or maybe I'm having this fight because now that I've discovered that the more of myself I cover, the better I look, I don't want to give it up.

* * *

So we're down to it. This evening I'm meeting with Coach
and a few of the first-stringers at the Chief Cafe to see if we
can talk some sense into me. Practice starts tomorrow; all
the slack is pulled tight. Coach picked the guys he wanted
to come: John Strate, our center and middle linebacker,
whose butt I have been nuzzled up under on offense for
three years; Tom Blackburn, a guard on both sides of the
ball, who has been protecting me for that same amount of
time; Elroy Crockett, an end who has been the recipient of
many a long bomb. Rich Dryden will be there, too. Like I
said, he's the second-string quarterback (unless we don't
come to a friendly resolution), and I suppose Coach wants
me imagining him in my place. I'm taking Ralph, just to
balance things out, and Grandma too, because Mrs.
McMurty can't stay with her tonight. That doesn't add up
to a lot of persuasive power, but how could Coach kick a
guy off the football team in front of his seriously whacked
grandmother?

"So, Mrs. Grayson, think Coach'll just let Benny stick
his hair up under his helmet an' pertend it's all cut? That's
what I'd do, I'd do it for sure. No see, no problem. Outta
sight, outta mind. So, Mrs. Grayson, did you get much of a
chance to talk to Benny about all this stuff?"

Ralph was present on one of those rare occasions
when Grandma snaps out of it and talks like she's never
been gone. He decided she hears everything and *chooses*
when to talk, like he wishes he could do. He chatters on
as we roll into town and pull up in front of the restaurant.

Coach and the guys are at the back table where we have the team breakfast every Friday before a game. Rich Dryden nods at Ralph. "What's *he* doing here?"

I say, "He's my date," and then have to convince Ralph I'm kidding. I ease Grandma into the empty seat next to Coach, who nods and says, "Hello, Mrs. Grayson," to the same response Ralph has been getting all evening.

Elroy, short and quick and *so* elusive, my favorite target, smiles and nods toward Dryden. "You're not going through with this, are you, buddy? I can't run slow enough to catch his balls."

Strate says, "Yeah, man, this is our year."

I look at them carefully, feel the pull. Like I said, I'm not real close with anyone, but I've played ball with these guys since junior high. The entire school, the *town* knows this is our year, so I definitely feel an obligation; plus it would be *my* championship, too. I glance up at the wall mirror behind them, see how my entire look is softened with the thick dark hair covering my mangled ears. I'm still no Steve McQueen, but damn.

"I'm not backing down on this, Benny," Coach says. "It's too important."

Coach knows a lot about football, but he's not the smartest guy I've run into. I decide to keep the ball in his court. "Tell me why it's so important."

"Come on, Benny, don't play dumb with me. You know football is a game of discipline."

"I do know that," I say. "Tell me one guy who's more disciplined than I am. I've played ball for you four years; never missed a curfew, never taken a drink of alcohol, never puffed a cigarette, never reported in anything but top shape."

"We've been over this," Coach says. "You're the quarterback, the team leader. Your appearance is a reflection on the team."

Hell with it, I'm gonna push him. "I understand that, too. Remember last year when you guys decided we needed to wear a tie and jacket on all road trips? You think I had a tie and jacket? Man, I can barely afford to feed myself and my grandma. I missed meals so I could 'reflect' the right image."

"Well," he says, "this one won't cost you anywhere that much. A buck twenty-five."

Strate says, "Hell, I'll spring for it."

I tell John I appreciate it, and I think he knows I don't. "Coach, tell me what you think will happen if you guys let me leave my hair like it is."

"I'm not going to get into this. . . ."

"Humor me, Coach. Who knows, maybe this time it'll take."

Coach takes a deep breath. "It sends a message that the rest of the team can do any damn thing they want. First it's hair, then . . . who knows what."

"Not me," I say. "I don't know what." I turn to Strate. "Truth, John. If they let me play this way, would you grow your hair long?"

"Hell, no. I'm no hippie."

"Rich?"

Rich shakes his head. "I don't want anybody mistaking *me* for a girl."

I look at Coach and shrug. "Who knows what?"

And he lets go. "You listen to me, you little smart-ass.

Don't pretend you don't know what that hair symbolizes. The longhairs are trying to tear the system down, and as long as there's a breath in my body, it won't happen on my watch. This is my football team, and if you want to play on it, you'll do what I tell you to do."

Ralph is wide-eyed, staring at Coach's pulse pounding in his temple. The other guys look embarrassed. Meekly, Elroy says, "Benny, come on, man. You're not going to throw away our season because of this."

"Why don't you ask your coach that question?" Grandma looks at Elroy, eyes clear as a bell.

Elroy is startled. "What?"

"Why don't you ask your coach if *he's* willing to throw away your season?" Grandma says. I'm stunned into silence.

"With all due respect, Mrs. Grayson—"

"If you want to show due respect, Mr. Greene, show it to my grandson." She turns to me. "Benny, let's go home. You're not going to get anywhere. He was thick when he was a boy and he's thick now."

Ralph jumps up. "No! Come on, Coach. Mrs. Grayson is right! Please! You could make it okay. You could just say it's okay and Benny could stick it up under his helmet! Please! I want Benny to hand me the ball!"

Coach shoots a disgusted look at Grandma, then at me. "Well, I hope you two are happy."

I feel it slipping away. Grandma stands and hobbles toward the exit. I follow, with Ralph close behind.

It is truly hard to know what to do with all this, hard to figure out the selfish part from the righteous part. I have forever measured my life by the athletic seasons, found my identity in what I could do with my body. But I'm also a student of history, and I know things don't change without someone going first. It ain't the hair, it's the control. When I was a little kid and the style was a crew cut or a flattop or even hair long on top but off the ears, I remember wishing I were a girl; that's how far I would have gone to be able to hide. I never imagined then that fashion would someday load the dice my way. Once I knew it, I couldn't *not* know it. I watched the Beatles' hair get longer and longer and dreamed of the sixties coming into Coyote Creek and freeing me. But my looks aside, men like Coach Greene have put more meaning into athletics than there ever should be, somehow believing team sports is holding up the empire or some damn thing. These are interesting times.

I'm going to miss football, and I feel as if I've betrayed Ralph. He'll be scared without me there to help, and Rich Dryden will ride him hard. Ralph is the one guy who could have made me reconsider, but after the night at the Chief, he told me to get out, that they'd never be fair to me. And he said something else. He said, "I know why you want to grow your hair, Benny. If I could grow my hair and make me not look dumb, I'd do it."

Sacrifices are being made all over the place. Cassius Clay changed his name to Muhammad Ali and declared himself a Muslim; in the United States of America, he was stripped of his title because of his *beliefs*. I'd feel more righteous about this if I were a pretty boy, but I'll make do. You read about the freedom to express yourself in your own U.S. government book, then turn around and have that freedom taken away because a coach or a principal feels he will lose control.

"Benny Woods, what are you doing on the sideline? You injured? I have my entire defense rigged to stop you."

I'm standing on the sideline at the first home game, talking to Coach Sixkiller, from Lodgepole. He fields a good team year after year even though they have fewer students than most teams due to the school's heavy Indian population. Their season starts a week later than ours, so he's scouting our game.

"Naw, not injured," I say, and tell him why I'm watching.

He stands back and appraises my appearance. His thick hair falls over his shoulders in braids. "They call that long?" He smiles. "If I kicked the longhairs off my team, I wouldn't have a team. There is history to consider." He looks at me another second, frowns again. "Benny Woods is on the sidelines because he won't cut his hair? That's it. No all-night kegger?"

"No all-night kegger," I say.

He motions me closer, whispers in my ear.

It's the last game of the season. I look through the window across the field at Coyote Creek's players streaming onto the field, jogging its length, and breaking into lines in the end zone for calisthenics. Without me, they are undefeated. I see Ralph, feel a tug in my heart.

Now I explode from my bus with my Lodgepole teammates, erupting in an ancient Indian war cry, knowing I owe my new teammates the respect of learning about that cry, about their tribes and their histories. They have given me sanctuary. My grandmother sits in the bleachers staring into space, surrounded by new friends who revere her for her years. Silky black hair spills from beneath the back of the helmet in front of me. We, too, are undefeated, and today I get the chance to prove myself.

Chris Crutcher

Having attended a small high school in Cascade, Idaho, Chris Crutcher knows firsthand the difficulties of putting together successful athletic teams with limited numbers of students. He himself ran track and played football and basketball. Like Benny, he says he had no choice.

A somewhat rebellious teenager himself during the 1960s, Chris Crutcher grew up to become first a successful child and family therapist and then one of the country's most highly regarded writers of fiction for teenagers. Every one of his six sports-oriented novels—*Running Loose, Stotan!, The Crazy Horse Electric Game, Chinese Handcuffs, Staying Fat for Sarah Byrnes,* and *Ironman*—as well as *Athletic Shorts,* his book of short stories—has been voted a Best Book for Young Adults by the American Library Association. The ALA, in fact, lists both *Stotan!* and *Athletic Shorts* among the 100 Best of the Best Books for Young Adults published between 1967 and 1992.

Chris Crutcher is also the recipient of the ALAN Award from the Assembly on Literature for Adolescents of the National Council of Teachers of English for his outstanding contributions to the field of young adult literature, and in 1998 the National Council of Teachers of English and SLATE (Support for the Learning and Teaching of English) named him the winner of the prestigious National Intellectual Freedom Award.

Seeing how much the screenwriter, director, and producers of the movie *Angus* changed his very popular short story "A Brief Moment in the Life of Angus Bethune," Chris Crutcher has opted to write the screenplays for *Staying Fat, Running Loose,* and *Crazy Horse,* though none has yet been filmed. In the meantime, he has finished a new novel called *Whale Talk* in which a young, disenfranchised student with nothing to lose walks into his classroom with a gun and changes the lives of his fellow students, and his own life, forever.

1970 - 1979

Although the 1970s lacked a dominant focus, the decade made up for that with its diversity. The social upheavals of the sixties died down with the end of American involvement in Vietnam and the political advances of African Americans and Hispanics. Women continued to make inroads into previously all-male domains, including politics, the military, and the church. And less frenzied space exploration continued with additional investigations of the moon, as well as long-term experiments in orbiting space labs and unmanned probes of nearby planets.

Environmental concerns resulted in the first efforts to reduce automobile emissions, passage of the Endangered Species Act, the control of toxic wastes, the investigation of damage to Earth's protective ozone layer, and attention to global warming.

The seventies was also when microchips and microprocessors were born, leading to the creation of pocket calculators, personal computers, computer games, videocassettes, video recorders, compact discs, and computer-controlled robots, along with satellite phone service, bar codes, magnetic phone cards, and the Sony Walkman.

The most important political event was the Watergate scandal, which resulted in the resignation of President Richard M. Nixon in 1974 and contributed to a growing awareness of the human failings of American heroes.

The unsettled nature of the times was reflected in American and British music, with rock and roll, country, and pop competing for attention with heavy metal, punk rock, reggae, and disco.

In the tongue-in-cheek story that follows, Bruce Brooks cleverly captures the unconventionality of the decade's lifestyles and identity by looking at one family's attempts to keep up with the times.

Do You Know Where Your Parents Are?

by Bruce Brooks

I put down my fork, having forced down the last three bites of my organic kale.

"Good boy," said my mother, peering at my empty plate through the light of the patchouli candle in the middle of the table my father had built. It leaned seriously to one side and wobbled on a short leg, but no one seemed to mind except me. "You ate a good dinner," my mother said. "Now just smoke your hash and then you may be excused."

"I don't *want* to smoke any hash," I said. "I have algebra homework—factoring quadratic equations. I need a clear head. I've told you a thousand times—getting whacked makes me woozy."

"You, like, heard your mother," said the incredibly soft voice of my father. I glanced over at him. Tonight he was dressed as, I think, a Chippewa—feathers, face paint, the works. But his eyes were full of stoned-out gravity.

"Oh, all right," I said with a heavy sigh. I smoked my hash. But I only pretended to inhale.

I read a book last summer in which the author smugly dismissed the artificial idea of marking time by decades. Nevertheless, there *were* what everyone calls "the sixties." The trouble is, most of what they mean by "the sixties" didn't start happening until about 1968 or so. Pretty late in the decade, if you think about it. For most of the *real* sixties, hip people weren't listening to Hendrix and the Jefferson Airplane and Moby Grape—they were listening to the Kingston Trio and Duane Eddy and the Smothers Brothers.

Also, my parents were not exactly avant-garde. They didn't catch on right away when things around them started to resemble the musical *Hair* a little bit. In the early sixties, I remember my mother changing every afternoon from a crisply pressed apron into a crisply pressed dress to greet my dad as he came home from work at the Office. She then served us meals composed almost entirely of canned goods (the miracles of science), from recipes she got out of magazines like *Family Circle* and *Good Housekeeping*.

Then, all of a sudden, she was supposed to be wearing flimsy granny skirts with little mirrors sewn into the fabric, and Indian cotton blouses without a brassiere underneath, and fringed ankle boots or—better yet—no shoes at all. My dad was supposed to drop the natty London Fog windbreaker with the elastic waist and the two-button collar snapped up and the Ban-Lon and the Weejuns for shabby denim bib overalls with sewn-on patches saying things like

FREE BOBBY SEALE and MAKE LOVE NOT WAR, worn over a T-shirt with a red fist or a portrait of Karl Marx on it. The large briar pipe containing Prince Albert was out; the teeny redwood pipe containing ganja was in.

Hey, it was a big jump, from "Michael, Row the Boat Ashore" to "Foxy Lady" overnight, or from an apron with Scottie dogs frisking on it to a tie-dyed granny dress. But my parents, once they saw what was going on in the culture, tried to catch up as well as they could. Before anyone knew it or acknowledged it, we were all past 1970, and the 1960s, as *years*, were history. But as a *concept*, as a *lifestyle*, the sixties were just taking hold of people like my mom and dad.

For example, in 1971 my parents officially changed all of our names. She used to be Frieda, Dad was Al, I was Al junior. Now she was registered simply as Snow, with no last name. My father cleverly went for a verb that had also become a kind of argot conjunction, meaningless but indispensable: His new name was Like.

They saved the worst for me. I, believe it or not, am now officially Yellow Submarine. My friends, after the inevitable period of mockery, just started calling me Sub. At my previous school, most of them had names like Richard or Mark. At the school to which I am bused crosstown this year, where I am, incidentally, one of 24 white students among 850 people my parents are pleased to call "Afro-Americans," my friends have names like Alonzalonzo and Al-Bokawiti. So my name doesn't sound especially gonzo to them, and they are good about taking it in stride.

Still, *they* do not have to bring marijuana-spiked brownies to school in their lunch bags, to eat after they finish the organic avocado and bean-sprout sandwiches on seventeen-grain bread, washed down with a Thermosful of carrot juice that sometimes has a psilocybin mushroom or a bud from a mescal cactus floating in it for "kick." Their mothers or big sister pack them PBJs, and that's that. What I wouldn't give for a PBJ. Except a spiked brownie—I make it a point of honor never to share the dope with which my mother feels she needs to indoctrinate me, or just give me that extra "kick" for the afternoon.

Speaking of kick, it so happens that our school has a terrific football team. And it so happens that despite the fact that I am white and often heavily drugged, I am quite swift of foot, deceptive of motion, and can really catch the old pigskin when it is flung anywhere near me. At least I discovered all this when, on kind of a perverse instinct, I went to the first couple of football scrimmages, and—surprise!—it looked as if I would make the team as a probable first-string wide receiver. But when I took home some medical-release forms for my parents to sign, they refused.

My father explained to me, "Competitive sports, man, are, like, symbols of totally unholistic warfare behavior. You know—like, the same kind of aggressive attitude that has the pigs bombing Laos with B-52s and assassinating the presidents of South American democracies and beating peaceful no-nuke protesters over the head with, like, truncheons and stuff."

"Pigs?" I said. "You mean, such as the ones who helped you change your tire on the side of the freeway in the snowstorm last winter? Or the ones who caught the junkie who ripped Mom's bag off her shoulder and ran up an alley in June?" I decided not to add that nobody had bombed Laos for several years.

My father might have flushed, but it was hard to tell because my mother had painted large pink peace signs on his cheeks and forehead during their regular Thursday acid trip. "Like, the answer is negativo, son— totally uncool on the football thing. Find, like, a sport where you don't have to, like, *win* over somebody, which can seriously undermine his self-esteem and stuff—a sport that's *positive*. That *supports* the nature of life, man. Competition doesn't support anything but more competition. Dig?"

I brought the unsigned forms back to school. During lunch that day I was hanging my head pretty low, and it wasn't because my mother had included a cookie spiked with bits of Quaalude (I never ate such delights). My buddy Lorenzal asked me what was wrong.

I looked at Lorenzal. His dad was an attorney. Lo was wearing khaki pants that had been ironed probably yesterday, a blue-striped shirt with a button-down collar, a red tie with blue toads on it, a black blazer, white socks, and black loafers. I was wearing acid-washed blue jeans, high-top black Chuck Taylor basketball shoes with purple laces, no socks, a gray sweatshirt with the multicolored Grateful Dead walking bears going around it, and a leather golfer's cap such as the one Bob Dylan made popular on one of his album covers. I shook my head at Lo.

"My folks say I can't play football," I said. "They wouldn't sign my health forms."

"Why won't they let you play?" said Lo. He loved the game, and from the first couple of scrimmages seemed destined to become a dynamite first-string cornerback. "What the heck is wrong with football? A pig was killed to make the ball or something?"

"It's competitive," I said. "Beating another team might lower the self-esteem of its players."

"Damn *straight*," said Lorenzal. "Grind that self-esteem right into the grit and *mud* with we big old nasty steel-tipped cleats. Send those boys home wetting they sorry *pants* on the bus and wondering if maybe next year they run cross-country or join the *Latin* club."

"They want me to play something 'holistic,' " I said. "Something 'in tune with nature.' "

Lo thought for a minute, rubbing the little patch of hair he grows beneath his lower lip until his father notices it every Saturday morning and makes him shave it off. "Well, you know, you *could* go out for the famous champion gardening team," he finally said.

"Thanks a lot, Lorenzal," I said bitterly.

"No, I'm serious. Just forge the initials on the forms, go ahead and *play* football, but tell the folks you're doing something else, like gardening, during practice and game times. *They'll* never know—why would *they* ever come to a football game and see you?"

I thought about it. "You're right. They would never support such 'warlike' activities with their attention, much less with the money it takes to buy tickets."

He spread his hands. "Man, you're a *natural* wide-out. You'll *start*, Sub. Think of it all: the awed respect of your fellow males. The dewy adoration of your female colleagues-in-education. And if you want me to get institutionally corny, I'll do it—the *school* needs you, dude."

I forged the signatures. I told my parents I had joined a club that would be planting the bulbs of perennial flowers throughout the fall and doing other landscaping work later on. Then every afternoon and Saturday morning I went out and seriously bashed some heads on the football field as a natural wide-out, true to Lorenzal's prediction, scattering inadequately matched bodies to the right and left as I sped, cut, leapt, and snatched, trailing in my wake a wreckage of self-esteem upon which I never looked back. Alone among our receivers I volunteered to run patterns that crossed the middle of the field, and when a cornerback or safety tried to stick me, I kneed him in the chin and left him for dead. Without paying attention, I led the team in receptions and touchdowns. I *humilated* defenders. I was a natural, a *star.* I was *the* star.

Maybe there was something to that organic kale after all. Following my first practice, I threw away all my mom's little narcotic "treats" except for a few painkillers I kept in my helmet in case a teammate was injured. I didn't need to be told the dope would hurt my hand-to-eye, slow me half a step, take the edge off my cut. But in front of my parents at home I kept pretending to be blown out.

Actually, I didn't have to pretend much, because almost as soon as football started, my parents began spending almost every evening out, at what they said was a class in weaving uncured goat's wool at a local artisan's studio. Usually I was in bed when they got home. Sometimes I heard my dad humming weird music as they came up the driveway from the VW bus, but my mother always shushed him before they got close to the house.

Only once, at breakfast, when I was yawning after a very strenuous practice the day before, did my mom ask how the gardening was going.

"Great," I said. "We were moving juniper bushes yesterday, and those things are *heavy.*"

"Take care not to disalign your chakras," she said.

"Will do," I said.

I couldn't believe it—football season had gone without a hitch, I had become a valiant if weirdly named member of my class, one with whom huge numbers of kids were chummy, and my parents were none the wiser. I felt as if what I had done in football would carry me through the year in something a lot more like a normal lifestyle than I could have hoped for before. Plus, contrary to my dad's warnings, I had *not* become a violent macho pig. I just loved catching passes.

Alas, I caught one too many. In the last game, a free safety hit me while I was twisted in the air for a ball thrown behind me. I landed funny and felt my femur pop. I was in the end zone, and I held on to the ball, setting a new school record for TDs in a season. From my helmet lining I took the four Percocets I had been saving for a teammate and crunched them myself, so the pain was minimal. But the school authorities had to call an ambulance to take me to the hospital, hopelessly bound in my dirty uniform. I left the stadium a hero to a standing O, but all I could think about was that the doctors in the emergency room would have to call my parents. And I wasn't dressed for moving juniper bushes.

* * *

For a full second, when my parents stepped into my cubicle in the emergency room, I really had no idea who was more embarrassed, them or me. I was in the muddy and obviously well-used uniform of a sport they had expressly forbidden me to play. But them! It was as if I had swallowed a month's worth of mescaline at once! My father was wearing an off-white jacket and pants, a long-collared, very shiny crimson shirt unbuttoned to the point just above where his small paunch started, three circular golden medallions, and black shoes with three-inch platforms beneath the sole and heel. If I had wanted to think about it—I did *not*—I might have concluded he was wearing a little eye makeup as well.

My mother was dressed more simply, in a flowing knee-length dress made of metallic silvery spangles, fastened over her shoulders by two little silver strings. Her shoes were silver, too. And, oh yes, my father was holding an immense three-tiered trophy made of gold and wood, with a dancing couple in golden metal on the top.

"Um," said my dad, "bummer about, like, the leg. Are you in pain?" He looked at my mom. "Do we have any—"

She shook her head just as I assured them I was okay. My father looked back at me, embarrassed. "We, like, cut out the drugs as soon as we started doing this—this disco stuff. The steps can get pretty tricky, and if you're whacked—"

"I gave it all up once football started, for the same reason," I said. "I threw the dope away at lunch."

He nodded, and there was an awkward silence. "So the weaving lessons?" I finally asked. "I won't be getting a sweater for Christmas that smells like feta cheese?"

My dad scratched his head. "Well, your mom was always

a great dancer, *great* body movement, back when dancing was just, like, cutting loose half naked at a rock concert or whatever, and, well, we were looking for something a little *different* to do together—"

"You took lessons," I said. "Every evening. That's where you went." I laughed. "Then you entered a competition."

My dad looked at the trophy in his hand as if he'd never seen it before, but my mother said, "Our very *first* competition. *And we kicked their butts!*"

"Yeah," said my dad, "we, like, won."

The doctor came in, managed to give my parents only the briefest of second looks, and said to me, "We need to set that leg and get a cast on it, young man."

As the doctor was wheeling my gurney out the door, I couldn't help saying, "What about the self-esteem of all those couples you beat?"

"What about it?" snorted my mother. "They would have trashed *ours* just as fast as they could."

My father cast her a glance and spoke more gently. "See, we thought about all of that. Right after we told you not to play football, in fact. And, like, we realized—animals compete for food, bands compete for contracts. Guys, like, compete for girls, babies compete for attention. If you *want* to, you can talk yourself into seeing, like, well, that *competition* is as much the nature of things now as, like, sharing was supposed to be a few years ago."

"And it *feels* better," my mother exulted, throwing her head back and raising both fists in the air. "We *slaughtered* them tonight! Passing a pipe never gave me a rush like *that*!"

The doctor cleared his throat and said, "He should be

ready within two hours. Not for competition—for going home to bed."

"Tell you what," my dad said to me as we left the room. "We'll just swing by the school field and see if you guys won the game, okay?"

"Cool," I said. "We were up fourteen, fourth quarter. Score ought to still be on the scoreboard."

He nodded. Then, as a last thought, he took the dancing trophy and tucked it under my blanket. The doctor must have slipped me an injection somewhere, because my eyes were closing, but just before they did, I read on the plaque that the award was made out to AL AND FRIEDA, FREESTYLE. Maybe there was hope.

Bruce Brooks

Bruce Brooks grew up in North Carolina during the 1960s and completed college at the University of North Carolina at Chapel Hill in 1972. He earned a Master of Fine Arts at the University of Iowa Writers' Workshop in 1980. Before becoming a successful novelist, he was a newspaper reporter, magazine writer, movie critic, and teacher.

In 1984 he introduced himself to an appreciative audience of librarians, teachers, and teenage readers with the publication of his first novel, *The Moves Make the Man*. This story of the friendship between two boys—a talented African American seventh-grader and a troubled white classmate—was not just good, but also won almost every major award for fiction, including a Newbery Honor, a *Boston Globe–Horn Book* Award, and a Best Book for Young Adults from the American Library Association. It is now considered one of the 100 Best of the Best Books for Young Adults published between 1967 and 1992.

Other high-quality, award-winning novels, with unusual characters and thought-provoking conflicts, followed: *Midnight Hour Encores, No Kidding, Everywhere,* and *What Hearts*. Along the way Brooks also published four nonfiction books about animals and natural science: *On the Wing: The Life of Birds; Nature by Design; Predator!;* and *Making Sense: Animal Perception and Communication,* as well as a collection of essays about such topics as winning, respect, bullies, friends, and caps called *Boys Will Be* and, with NBA basketball star Glenn "Doc" Rivers, *Those Who Love the Game.*

More recently, Bruce Brooks has written a series of lively novels for younger male readers about a hockey team, each story focusing on a different player, called The Wolfbay Wings.

1980 - 1989

Although America and much of the industrialized world fell into a recession at the start of the 1980s and there were more homeless people in America than at any other time since the Great Depression fifty years earlier, life throughout the world continued in much the same way as in prior decades. There were, for example, major disasters such as floods in Bangladesh, a drought in Ethiopia and Sudan, a meltdown at the Chernobyl nuclear plant in Ukraine, a huge oil spill off the coast of Alaska, and the first warnings of an AIDS epidemic.

Terrorist hijackings and bombings increased worldwide, and American hostages were taken from the U.S. embassy in Tehran, Iran. During the decade, the president of Egypt and the prime minister of India were assassinated, and both Pope John Paul II and President Ronald Reagan were wounded in assassination attempts. And in

Beijing, China, the military, using rifles and tanks, opened fire on unarmed students in Tiananmen Square who had been demonstrating peacefully for democratic reforms.

By the end of the decade, reforms in the Soviet Union resulted in the overthrow of Communist rule throughout Eastern Europe and the dismantling of the hated Berlin Wall.

But for reasons unknown, some Americans, especially young people, had become fairly complacent and more self-centered than those in earlier decades. One of the most unusual things done by a teenager during this decade occurred in 1987 when a nineteen-year-old West German named Mathias Rust flew a four-seater Cessna across heavily defended Soviet airspace without being detected. Reaching Moscow, he circled the Kremlin and landed his plane in Red Square. Using that event as background in the story that follows, Chris Lynch explores the self-centeredness of some American teenagers at that time.

Rust Never Sleeps

by Chris Lynch

"Who?"

"Ingo Rust."

"Stop pulling my chain. Where's the clicker?"

"I'm serious, that's who's coming. Ingo Rust."

"I'm serious. Where's the clicker?"

"Doesn't anything excite you? This is like, history coming for a visit."

"The clicker excites me, Daphne. Gimme the clicker."

Daphne throws the remote the entire length of the sofa to Daniel. Daniel begins pounding his way up and down the channels.

"Why do you call it a clicker, anyway? It doesn't make any sound at all."

"It only talks to me. Just like you. Now could you be quiet, please?"

"Why? What's so important that you have to listen to it instead of me?"

"I'm watching this thing about the disappearing orangutans in Borneo . . . ah, the hockey game . . . ah, the weather . . . the orangutans . . . *Sesame Street* . . ."

"Right. You watch every damn thing that comes up, and you don't even know who Ingo Rust is."

Daniel blows a flume of exasperation toward the ceiling. "All right, all right, who is Ingo Rust?"

"He's German."

Daniel takes a brief look away from twenty-one inches of Sony Trinitron to stare sideways at his sister. "You interrupted amazing photos of Neptune's moon Triton to tell me that?"

"He's a German exchange student. He's going to be with us for six months. You know, in a way, Germany's the most important place in the world right now. And guess whose brother he is. Go on, guess."

Daniel is staring at a tennis match. "Ivan Lendl's."

"Lendl's not even German. He's a Czech."

"Shows you what *you* know. They happen to be the same thing."

"They are *not* the same thing, Daniel," Daphne says, throwing a pillow at the television. "And you are *such* an embarrassment, what with international visitors coming and everything."

"Hey, here's a joke I heard on Johnny Carson the other night. Ready? Okay, you know how East Germany decided to reunite with West Germany? Well, they liked that idea so much they decided to go ahead and reunite with Poland, too. Then Czechoslovakia. Then France . . ."

"Are you going to do this when he's here, Daniel? Because if you are going to parade your ignorance the whole time, I think we should exchange you to some other country for the duration."

"Make it Hawaii."

"Hawaii is not another country," she snaps.

"Fine, whatever you say. Who is Ingo's brother?"

"Ingo's brother is . . . Mathias Rust."

Daniel stares at her. She stares at him. He turns back to the television, where hundreds of volunteers are using rags to clean black oil off the millions of rocks of Prince William Sound.

"You don't know who he is."

"Of course I do. He's a swimmer, right? Banned for taking steroids and cutting through the water like a shark."

"Mathias Rust. The guy who flew the little plane from Finland through Soviet airspace and buzzed Moscow before landing right in Red Square?"

"Oh, ya, *that* Mathias Rust," Daniel says, nodding. "But he *was* on steroids, right?"

"Go on and mock, but you were very impressed at the time. You remember how old Mathias was?"

"I don't remember how old *you* are. Why would I care about him?"

"I'm seventeen. Mathias was nineteen. He did all that when he was only nineteen years old. Changed history, the son of a gun. Humiliated the whole military setup there in the Soviet Union, and Gorbachev took advantage of the situation to can these big defense ministry types, all because of little Mathias. Think about that, potato head. That boy did all that when he was just *your* age."

Daniel suddenly is seized: eyes wide and searching. He goes rigid, then bursts out of the chair. He is gone, then rapidly back again, S-shaped into his spot on the sofa before the cushions can even regain their puff. He tears open a big bag of nacho cheese Doritos.

"Okay, so who's this Gorbachev again?"

Daniel and Daphne are sitting at the international terminal at Logan. They are slumped into molded plastic seats that are covered in a thinly padded vinyl upholstery and stuck together with six other identical chairs. Staring nearly straight up, as if they've got the front-row seats at the movies, they watch the arrivals monitor. Their parents are in the lounge, sipping Beck's and madly poring over their Berlitz German phrase book.

"No, Daphne, I do get it. It was very brave. He's cool. But I still think he did it for money."

Daphne lets out a small growl. "You know, some people do things for other reasons besides money."

"True. Maybe he got laid."

Daphne calmly stands and walks the length of the row and takes the seat furthest from her brother. They talk across the six empties.

"Where's the clicker?" he says. "Throw me the clicker."

"Hey, look," Daphne says, all excited, "there's Ollie North—and he's got Fawn Hall with him."

Daniel springs out of his chair. "Where?"

"You are pathetic," she says.

"What? You lied to me? That's not funny! That's . . . that's . . . Christ, Daphne, that's Colonel North we're talking about. He's a hero, for God's sake . . . fought the whatchamacallits, the Contras . . ."

"You mean *supported* the Contras."

"Anyway, the good guys. He supported the good guys down there."

"By selling arms to Iran . . ."

"But to whack *Iraq*."

"You don't even know who Gorbachev is, and you get all excited about—"

"No, no. The difference is, one of them is a threat to democracy, and the other one is a champion of democracy."

"And one of them had a girlfriend pose in *Playboy*."

"See, you do understand."

Daphne sighs. She points up to the video screen. "Go back to your program."

The monitor shows that the flight from Hamburg is to be delayed another hour. Daniel lets out a loud moan. When his sister doesn't answer, he does it again. She shushes him and stares at the monitor, as if the story is climaxing.

"You know what we should do," he says brightly. Daniel doesn't do brightly very often. Not without artificial brightness enhancer, anyway.

She looks at him through slits.

"I think we need to show Ingo *Bright Lights, Big City*."

"Great. You read one book your whole life and it becomes your guiding philosophy."

"Wrong. I also read *Fox in Socks*."

"Better. Show him the *Fox in Socks* side of American life instead. At least it doesn't include drugs and puking and psychotic debauchery."

Daniel nods wisely. "It does if you look closely enough."

"Deviate," she sighs, then calmly sticks her fingers in her ears.

Daniel pulls them out. "Come on, Daphne, I'm only thinking of our guest."

"Not only are you not thinking of our guest, not only do you never think of anybody else—Dan, you don't even *believe* in thinking of others."

"It was a joke," he snaps. "I didn't write *Wall Street,* I just said it made more sense than the Bible."

"It was a *movie,* dumdum. Nobody but you *believed* the 'greed is good' speech."

"Fine. If I say greed is bad . . . ?"

"No."

"Come on, a little Bolivian marching powder and we'll have Rusty singing 'God Bless America' before he has a chance to unpack his little leather shorts."

She takes a deep breath. "Don't call him Rusty."

He stands. He walks to the big window, and as he does, a TWA jumbo jet backs away, as if Daniel is scaring it off.

"Let's make a run," Daniel says, hurrying back to her.

"No."

"Come on, we can be back with the stuff in plenty of time."

"No."

"They'll let you take the car. You know they'll let you take the car. They're drinking, and they like you. All you gotta do is ask."

"No."

"Good. Better. Don't ask. Just take the car. They love it when you do that sixties rebellion crap they don't have the energy for anymore."

"Fine, if it's such a great idea, then you do it."

"Right. Rebellion is one thing. Driving with a

suspended license is a costly thing. They don't support rebellion that costs money. Come on, Daph. Just once more . . . it'll be fun . . . nobody'll get hurt . . . and then I swear, on my soul, tomorrow—"

"We'll just say no," Daphne says morosely.

Daniel appears not to realize it, but he has managed to convince himself of the greatness of the idea. He liked it to begin with, yet he's all but salivating now. He has, however, left his sister behind.

"Not this time," she says firmly. "I think we should just say now. I mean, we should say no now. Or just say *nine*, in honor of our German guest."

He starts backing away. "Come along, girl. Leave Daphne here, waiting for Rusty, and let our old buddy Daffy out. Just for . . ." He looks at his watch. "Forty-five minutes. We'll be back by five."

"Don't go," she says.

"Come," he says.

"Stay," she says. "You're about to meet the brother of a hero. That'll be thrill enough."

Daniel makes a gesture like he's doing publicly something only monkeys normally do publicly. "He did it for the money, Daphne. Grow up."

"He didn't make any money. And he went to prison for over a year."

"He did it for the attention."

"He did it to promote peace. He did it to meet Gorbachev and talk about the possibility of disarmament."

"He did it to promote himself. He did it to meet chicks and talk about the possibility of sex."

Daphne stands up. There is no point in trying anymore. Instead she raises both hands high and starts chopping the air in her brother's direction, like the guys on the ground directing the planes.

"You know," he says sternly, "the money I'm going to have to spend on a cab has to come out of the money I was going to spend buying the shit, which directly reduces the amount of thrill I can purchase." He stares, convinced this will trouble her.

It doesn't. "Be back here by five, cement head, and meet a *real* man."

"What? You're kidding. President Bush is gonna be here, too?"

Daniel is back by five. Five A.M. He sits on the edge of Daphne's bed. When sitting down hard does not wake her, he stands and then sits down harder. Slowly she rolls over, blinks a couple of times. Daniel opens a big white smile on her, to match his now big white hair.

"You weren't missed," she says calmly, closing her eyes again.

He takes this as his cue, and he's off galloping at the mouth. "Of course I was," he says. "It must have been dead here without me. Dead. Wasn't dead where I was, though, wasn't dead at all, babe, should've been there, Daph. Wish you were there, Daph. How was it with Rusty? Was it embarrassing, Ma and Dad using up all their phrases in the first five minutes, like, 'Hello, Rusty. May I go to the toilet? Would you point me to the train station? Yes, I would love a hot dog. . . .' "

"Nobody spoke German. Ingo's English is better than yours."

"Hey, that's good. Ingo's English. That's what we'll speak now. Ingo's English. Hey. Check this out."

Daniel races over to Daphne's stereo.

"Leave that alone," she snaps. "You know what time it is?"

He waves her off and sticks a disc in the player. He spins the volume knob and in seconds the room is shaking.

If I had the chance I'd ask the world to dance
and not be dancin' with my-sel-elf . . .

Daphne hurls herself out of the bed and at the stereo. She punches the Power button, and the world outside Daniel's head goes dead silent.

Daniel goes on dancing with himself.

"This explains the look," she says, pointing at his head of bleached and spiked hair, his armless faux-leather jacket, his fingerless leather gloves and selection of cheap silvery rings, bracelets, and chains.

Daniel is pleased to be noticed. "I was at a Halloween party," he says.

"It's November, Dan."

"Who's telling this story, me or you? So anyway, my buddies, right, after a while decided that I looked a lot like Billy Idol. And so we did me up and . . . well, were they right, or what? Coincidentally, we found out when we went downtown that there was a Billy Idol night on at the Metro . . . and I goddamn *won*, can you believe it? I won this CD." He rushes back to the stereo, oblivious to being banned from it.

Daphne beats him by a step, slaps her hand over the Power button, and stands guard in front of it.

"And I also won a bottle of tequila, but I don't know where that is."

Daphne has her head half turned, as if looking at Daniel is hurting her eyes.

"Where are your clothes, Dan? You had a nice jacket on when you left, and now you're wearing plastic."

"Pffft," he says, looking at his new ensemble, licking his thumb and rubbing away a smudge of something from the high-sheen front of the jacket. "What I was wearing before was foof. That was Duran Duran Frankie Goes to Hollywood crap, and those guys were *right* to beat me up and take it away."

Daphne covers her eyes with her hand. "Just go crash, Daniel. Get yourself some sleep. You're going to need all your strength for feeling like a jackass later today."

"What're you, joking? I'm not going to bed. That party's just getting started."

She uncovers her eyes. "Oh, no," she says. "You just go right on back if you want to, but I'm not going anywhere. You leave me be." She dashes past him, jumps into bed, and pulls the covers up to her nose.

"Dream on, wallflower. I'm not here for you. I came to get Dingo."

"No," she insists.

"Yes," he insists. "I told these girls that I had Mathias Rust over here, and it was like *boom*—all eyes on me. Seems everybody knows our hero, and that translates to big-time action for ol' Billy here."

"No!" She leaps out of bed.

"Yes!" He pushes her back down.

Daphne is lying there, staring up at her brother with a look that is half horrified, half enraged.

"I'm sorry," he says, "I'm sorry. . . . That's not what I meant to do. . . ." He is fidgeting now, looking like he's lost the plan. He glances over to the stereo, then out the window, where the sun is coming up peach-colored and haze-haloed. He is grinding his teeth, licking his lips. "I'm sorry, Daph. I didn't mean that. Of course you are invited as well."

He turns and dashes out of the room, with Daphne hot behind him.

"You leave him *alone,*" she snap-whispers, but then she is stopped short, bumping smack into Daniel's back.

"Good morning," Ingo says quietly from the dining room table. "I'm sorry if I woke you. With the time difference and the jet lag, I could not sleep any longer."

Daniel hasn't got the patience to be stunned for very long.

"How old are you? I thought you'd be older."

"He's sixteen, Dan, and leave him alone."

Ingo rises from the table and scoots down the hall to his room.

"Now look what you did—you scared him. Ya freak."

Ingo is back quickly. He hands Daniel a knot of black cotton. "A pleasure to meet you, Daniel. I brought you something."

Daniel unfurls the gift, a T-shirt. He stares at it silently for several seconds, until Daphne tires of waiting and reads it aloud.

"It says 'International Airport, Red Square. Opening May 28, 1987.' Cool."

"What?" Daniel says. "Oh. Right. Cool."

Ingo shrugs. "My brother Mathias sent you that. My brother Mathias landed his plane in Moscow on that date.

He wants American teenagers to know about it. These shirts were very popular and very funny at the time of the flight. My brother Mathias went to jail."

Ingo sounds like a robot as he speaks. As he turns and walks back to his place at the table, Daniel looks over his shoulder at his sister. "I got the same thing," she whispers. "The shirt and the speech."

Ingo looks like the most polite customer in a diner, sitting there well-postured and expectant.

"Can I get you something to eat?" Daphne asks.

"If it is no trouble," he answers.

Daphne is most happy to do something for the guest. She heads straight for the kitchen, giving his shoulder a friendly squeeze on her way by. Ingo reacts to the touch as if it were a small, not unpleasant electrical charge. He stares, at the hand, then at the warm handprint that it left.

Daniel takes his seat across from Ingo.

"So, your brother's a hero, like."

"So he is."

"Big superstar in your country?"

"He was popular for a while when he got out of prison."

"How do you feel about that, having a rock-and-roll star for a brother?"

"Mathias flew from Helsinki across four hundred and twenty miles of Soviet airspace and landed in Red Square because he wanted to promote the cause of disarmament. He wished to speak with Mr. Gorbachev. It was a brave thing Mathias did, and he wishes to be a role model for American teenagers."

Daniel stares at Ingo. Daniel smiles. Ingo smiles back, but it is merely a facsimile. "Be with ya in a sec, Ingo."

In the kitchen, Daphne is frying up eggs and bacon. The scent, warmth, and feel of the very grease in the air swarms all over Daniel. "Damn, that smells good. I wish I could eat without vomiting."

"It's just as well you can't. It's for company."

"Ya, about *company*. I'm dying out here, Daphne. What's with him?"

"I don't know. He was just like that last night. He doesn't seem very happy, does he?"

"Think that's it? You think he's not happy to be here?"

Daphne moves from the frying pan to the toaster, pops in a couple of wheat slices. "Could be homesick, I guess."

Daniel's got his mandate. "Right," he says, marching back into the other room.

"Yo, Ingo," he says. He turns his chair around backward and leans forward on it, intimate-like.

"Yes?"

"You like drugs?"

"Daniel!" Daphne says, putting a cup of hot chocolate in front of Ingo.

Daniel waves her off.

"No, thank you," Ingo says, unfazed.

"How would you like to go to a party, pretend to be your brother, and have lots of sex with American girls?"

Daphne grabs her brother by his white hair and his vinyl jacket, wrestles him into the kitchen. "Cut it out," she says.

"Cut what out? I am going to make that boy happy."

"Bullshit. You don't care one bit about that boy's happiness. You're just using him as a prop for your own smutty thrills."

The grease in the pan is now burbling and sizzling

madly. Daphne looks at it, at the bacon getting overcrispy and the egg developing small, hard tumors. She shuts off the gas.

"You still don't get it, do you, Daph? The message of the age. Synchronicity, y'know, like the Police album. His happiness *is* my happiness, and my happiness is his happiness. Greed is good because it makes things happen, and Ronnie Reagan's whole thing with the jelly beans and everything trickling down so if, like, the top-feeders get to gorge, then the bottom-feeders get the bits that fall, and so, like, self-interest is, really, not selfish at all but is, in reality, a gesture of love to all mankind. See?"

Suddenly Daphne is holding the grease-filled frying pan. "You slimeball . . . you greasy low-life . . ."

Until Ingo breaks it up, speaking from the kitchen doorway.

"All right, but can I have my breakfast before I go? I would like my breakfast for my strength."

"My *man*," Daniel says, smiling broadly.

Daphne drops the pan back down on the stove, throws her hands in the air. She heads back to her bedroom. "You serve him," she says to Daniel.

"And so I will," Daniel says.

It takes roughly one minute for Ingo Rust to make his food disappear. Then he is gone into his room to prepare. In a short time he is back out, and transformed. His reddish blond hair, downy and flyaway a few minutes before, is now sleek and slicked straight back under the power of gel. His Mathias Rust T-shirt is gone now, replaced with a green velour V-neck jersey, black wool sport coat with shoulder pads the size of dachshunds, and baggy gray pleated pants.

He has in his hand a couple more crisply folded new Mathias Rust T-shirts.

"I think maybe these would be good to bring with us, no?" he asks a very anxious Daniel as they head out the door.

"Excellent," Daniel says. "You are gold, boy." He claps him on the back.

"You would really do this?" It is Daphne, standing, arms folded, behind them. "Ingo? You would really do this, pretending to be Mathias? Trading on his heroism? Just to get girls?"

Ingo is momentarily stopped. The sad look, which had briefly left him, is back. He looks down at his feet and appears for a second ready to change his mind again. Then he looks up and into her eyes.

"Mathias was never ashamed pretending to be Mathias. Why should I be?"

And before he can hear her response, or see it in her eyes, he looks again down at his feet. Then Daniel completes the scene.

"Don't wait up," he says, reaching over and closing the door between them.

It is late afternoon when Daphne shows up at the door of the apartment where she knows the party is. Where the party always is. She lets herself in, since the door is open. The door is always open. She walks through the rubble of glasses and ash trays and bottles and shoes. Through the aroma of dead tobacco and liquor and perspiration. There is one guy who looks even younger than Ingo, sleeping on the counter that separates the kitchen and living room. Two more guys, slightly older, sleep in their Calvin Klein briefs and new Mathias Rust T-shirts on the floor. Through the stereo, Lionel Richie greets Daphne with

> *Hello . . .*
> *Is it me you're looking for . . .*

while Billy Idol and Mathias Rust sleep soundly, sharing one couch head to foot.

"Mr. Rust has to go home," she says coldly, standing over them.

There is no response.

"Wake up. He has to go home, right now."

"Christ, Daphne," Daniel growls. He attempts to open his eyes, but the soft yellow light of the room is too harsh, so he closes them again. "Give us a break, will you? I'll bring him home in a while."

"I don't mean that home. I mean his home. Hamburg. His mother called, hysterical, and he has to go back. Something serious. Sickness in the family. She was very short about it, but he has to get back, right away."

Daniel starts rocking Ingo with his feet. "Kid. Hey, kid. You have to get up. You have to go. They need you at home."

Ingo does not appear to completely comprehend but instinctively rises to his feet. He wobbles. Daphne puts a hand on him and he steadies. He is rumpled and dazed, and his hair is a wild, rigid mess, arranged something like the Statue of Liberty's crown.

"I am sorry," Ingo says to her. She nods and rubs both of his arms up and down, up and down, massaging blood or energy, warmth, life back into him. "I am sorry," he repeats.

Daniel is asleep again as she leads Ingo out.

* * *

They sit staring, distantly, at the television six feet away.
Daniel flips the stations. The History Channel is doing
Churchill. A&E is doing *Cat on a Hot Tin Roof.* VH-1 is running its twenty-four-hour Madonnathon, which Daniel
watches for twenty-four seconds. He hits CNN.

*And 1987's teenage wonder, Mathias Rust, is back in the
news and back in trouble today, arrested in Germany for the stab-
bing of a female coworker at the Hamburg hospital where they were
both employed. It seems that twenty-one-year-old Rust assaulted the
woman after she had rejected his amorous advances. . . .*

"Where's the clicker?" Daphne says flatly. "What's on
MTV? I want the clicker. Throw me the clicker."

Daniel throws her the clicker.

Click.

"You're right," she says. "It does make a clicking sound.
I can hear it."

Daniel looks at her, channel-surfing.

He slides down to her end of the couch, leans his head
on her shoulder.

"For what it's worth, Daph, I'm sure he was a legit hero,
until he got into his twenties."

She continues to riffle through channels but now leans
her head on his. She pauses on *Sesame Street,* then moves on.

"Go back, go back," Daniel says. "Put it back to *Sesame Street.*"

Click.

"I always loved this, too," Daphne says brightly as Maria
sings "*Hola* means hello." Daphne adds, "This show always
reminds me of what's fine in the world."

"Ya," Daniel says. "Maria is *so* fine."

Click.

Chris Lynch

With his first novel, *Shadow Boxer,* Chris Lynch gained immediate attention as a significant writer for young adults. The novel explores the relationship between two brothers, the younger of whom wants to pursue a boxing career in spite of the fact that their boxer father died from injuries he received in the ring. Lynch followed that with *Iceman, Gypsy Davey,* and *Slot Machine,* all American Library Association Best Books for Young Adults as well as ALA Recommended Books for Reluctant Young Adult Readers.

In *Slot Machine,* Elvin Bishop is like so many teenage misfits: unable to fit the traditional roles expected of high-school males. He's murdered in football, smashed in base-ball, squashed in wrestling, but still struggles—fortunately, with a good bit of humor—to find a place where he can fit in. Readers who sympathize with Elvin are sure to want to read about how he handles his next challenge in the high-school social scene, a love affair, in *Extreme Elvin.*

In *Political Timber,* a satirical novel with a political slant, Chris Lynch introduces Gordon Foley, a high-school senior whose scheming grandfather (in prison for fraud) con-vinces him to run for mayor as well as senior-class presi-dent—with amusing results.

Lynch's most disturbing characters and conflicts appear in his Blue-Eyed Son trilogy: *Mick, Blood Relations,* and *Dog Eat Dog.* In those novels, Mick tries to escape the restrictions of his blue-collar, Boston Irish family, but his violent, hard-drinking brother and bigoted white neighbors continually place painful obstacles in his way.

Lynch's most recent book, *Whitechurch*, is a novel told in stories and prose poem, detailing the lives of a trio of teenagers as they struggle with existence in their northern New England town in the 1990s.

Lynch's characters are always interesting and their problems thought-provoking. Though their lives are often full of pain and turmoil, there is humor and hope in each of them.

For younger readers, Chris Lynch has written the He-Man Women Haters Club series, which includes *Johnny Chesthair, Babes in the Woods, Scratch and the Sniffs, Ladies' Choice,* and *The Wolf-Gang.*

he weather during the 1990s made more news than at any other time during the century. This decade had the five warmest years in weather history, with the highest average global temperature ever recorded. Weather extremes were common, one of which was "The Storm of the Century" during the winter of 1993 that affected twenty-six eastern states; later that same year, the flooding of the Mississippi and Missouri Rivers created a 20-million-acre lake over parts of several states. There were also weather disasters in Bangladesh, Papua New Guinea, India, and China, wildfires in California, and earthquakes in Japan and California.

Wars made news, too, especially in the Middle East, Somalia, Bosnia, and Yugoslavia, as did anti-American terrorism in Saudi Arabia, Kenya, Tanzania, and at home with the bombing of the World Trade Center in New York City. None of those things, however, were as shocking as the bombing of the Murrah Federal

Building in Oklahoma City by an American right-wing extremist. The growth of extremist groups, such as skinheads and underground militias, within the United States, in fact, was another significant feature of this decade.

But the most dominant force of the final decade of the twentieth century was the growth of the Internet, which has changed the way we share information and interact with one another. With the touch of a few computer keys, almost anyone can buy books or jewelry or even a car, play games, trace genealogies, do research for school assignments, communicate with authors, and chat with friends as well as complete strangers anywhere in the world. Although some adults remain fearful of the negative influences of the Net on young people, Alden R. Carter presents a more optimistic view of teenage communication in this collection's final story.

Y2K.CHATRM43

by Alden R. Carter

At the end of this story I'm supposed to turn off my computer and go outside to enjoy a beautiful autumn evening: the real world as opposed to cyberspace, reality as opposed to the electronic void, blah blah . . . Well, I guess we'll have to see what happens. But beginnings first.

The bus let us off at the corner of Marathon and Peach in the late October dusk. As usual, I walked the last couple of blocks to my street with Adrien Koudalakian, who's Lebanese-Armenian and looks it. We've never been boyfriend and girlfriend, just friends and neighbors for just about forever. I guess it's a condition that Adrien feels gives her the right to rip on me every so often—actually, pretty often. Tonight was one of those nights.

"You ought to get involved in some stuff, Joel," she snapped. "It'd give you a better attitude. Today in Mod Prob you were so depressing, I felt like hitting you with a textbook. A big, heavy one."

"Well, school violence is another modern problem we ought to discuss. Bring it up tomorrow."

She glared at me. "In your case a whack alongside the head would be therapy. How come you see the dark side of everything? This is going wrong, that's falling apart, disaster is right around the corner. You're a gloomy Gus."

"That's an old one," I said.

"I know. That's what my grandma calls my grandpa when he starts in on how the world's going to hell."

"He's probably got a point."

"Oh, pooh. There are lots of reasons to be optimistic about the future."

"Name a dozen and I'll name two dozen why you're wrong."

She turned on me, stamping a foot she was so mad. "Just take a break, will you? Get away from your computer. Get out of your dumb chat room and spend some time around real people. I remember when you used to be in band and lots of things. Now you're gone in hyperspace every spare minute you've got."

"Cyberspace, not hyperspace."

"Whatever. The point is, all you do anymore is play with your computer."

She'd finally hit a nerve. "I don't *play* with my computer! I *use* it. And, by the way, how's that new Power Mac I helped you set up last summer?"

"It's fine! And I get your point. But there's a difference: I use my computer to get my homework done so I can get on to other things. You? You almost live on the Web."

"So? It happens to be what I like to do. And don't tell

me my chat room is dumb. We're doing important stuff there. We're trying to solve some problems."

"Yeah, yeah. You told me all about your chat room. Trying to solve the problems of the twenty-first century while there's still time. But three hours every night, Joel? Don't you get depressed worrying about the world's problems every night?"

I glared at her. "Yeah, I get depressed about the world's problems, Adrien. But at least I'm doing something about them. Or trying to."

She returned the glare and then huffed off. I went in to help with supper.

My parents argued all the time we were eating. At least the subject wasn't money or Dad's drinking or what's going to happen to Grandpa Mel (Mom's dad) or Grandma Fran (Dad's mom) when they can no longer live on their own. Instead, they were back on Dad's essay.

Mom, who's got a double master's in history and linguistics but sells real estate, slapped her napkin down hard enough to make the ice in the glasses rattle. "Franklin!" (She only calls Dad Franklin when she's really mad.) "You cannot mix French and German in the same sentence! 'Fin-de-millénaire angst' may sound just wonderful to you, but other professors are going to jump down your throat! And you should know it."

Dad tried to adopt his amused, professorial look, but the tic below his left eye gave him away. Dad used to be a tenured sociology professor at the university until Auren Products hired him away to do demographic and market analysis. Five years of big bucks and good times for the family. But last spring a German conglomerate, Bettelheim Limited, swallowed Auren. Then came the big sweat to squeeze costs and maximize profits. And guess what? Demographic and market analysis performed by Dr. Franklin Sandley became a frill. Bye-bye job, hello major panic in the Sandley household.

Dad had enough pull to get back on the faculty part-time, but he's got to impress some people and do it fast to win a full-time appointment. Hence the essay. He cleared his throat, still hoping the professorial approach would work. "No, Kit. I cannot agree. As you know better than anyone, English borrows from every language and mixes the results higgledy-piggledy. Now just imagine if this becomes a major catchphrase. If *Newsweek* or *Time* were to pick it up, my career could be remade in a week."

I was tempted to ask if we'd then become *millénaire* mil-lionaires, but held myself back. This was serious. Dad had already explained to me (with his usual pained expression at my ignorance) that *fin de millénaire* meant "end of the mil-lennium." I knew what *angst* meant. "Why don't you just call it Y2K anxiety?" I said. "That would do it, and it's catchy."

They ignored me, as usual. "Higgledy-piggledy, piggledy-higgledy, I don't care!" Mom snapped. " *Fin-de-millénaire angst*'doesn't have a word of English in it."

I sighed and shrugged. So much for the peacemaking biz. And I'd wasted a good idea, too. I finished my lasagna, put the plate in the dishwasher, and went down to open the chat room.

I guess this brings me to the point where I have to explain how I became a Webdict. (Web plus addict. Clever, huh?) It's not much of a story. I just dig the Web and have since the first time I got on a computer powerful enough to really cruise. For a long time I was happy jumping from one chat room or newsgroup to the next. (I guess Adrien could call me a hyper cybersurfer if she ever got her terms straight.) But after a few months the stupid talk in the chat rooms really started to irritate me. I mean, I could go all over the Web, learning stuff that was happening all over the world. But when I went to a chat room to talk about it, here were these people flaming each other just for the heck of it: "suck my toe jam"; "eat my shorts"; "hey the snot you just sneezed was really your brains man."

Just junk like that. And stupid me, I decided to try to do something different: I opened Y2K.CHATRM43.

Y2K.CHATRM43 is supposed to discuss the problems of the new millennium. Rules: teenagers only; keep to the nightly topic; serious comments only; don't monopolize; keep your mind open; no flaming.

Amazingly, the chat room caught on. Not that it was any big fad or anything, but a lot of people stopped by. Most only hung around a few minutes, dropped a comment or two, and then cruised off into cyberspace. But a few stayed and kept coming back night after night. Most of the regulars were from around the U.S., but we had quite a few international log-ins despite the problems of language and time zones. In all, I counted some thirty countries over the course of six months. A few of the logins might have been fakes. (One kid from North Carolina claimed to be from Tahiti until we caught him in a lie.) Still, I was pretty sure that most of them were for real.

For quite a while the rules actually worked. Cyberpunks

would check through, decide we were boring, drop an obscene comment or two, and then boost off for the next chat room. We'd go back to business. Our discussions didn't find magic solutions to anything big. We didn't find any way to defuse the population bomb, close the hole in the ozone layer, end terrorism, or cure AIDS. Still, we talked through a lot of things.

But after a few months all the talk about big, big problems without any solutions started getting big-time depressing. I don't know what I expected. Were we going to wow the United Nations with some radical and painless solution to a problem? Were we going to find a magic bullet to shoot one of the world's really nasty werewolves? No, I don't think any of us were that naive. But when nothing new happened, people started losing interest. A lot of the regulars just dropped out. Those who remained started wanting to talk more and more about smaller and smaller issues: tattooing, dating, clothes, school rules, getting along with parents.

Hard as I tried as the chatmaster, I couldn't keep them on the nightly subjects for very long. I wasn't about to admit it to Adrien, but she was right: The chat room was taking far too much of my time and leaving me depressed just about every minute of the day. I had to break free, but it was tough. I'd had a lot of hopes and it was hard to let them go.

Logging on to my server, I told myself that maybe tonight would be better, that maybe tonight I'd find enough reason to go on believing. But I wasn't really hopeful. No, this was it. Time to shut down Y2K.CHATRM43 while I still had something like a life.

I'd set up the evening's question the night before: *What do you see as the future of international peacekeeping? When should NATO, the UN, or other international organizations deploy armed forces?*

The subject was a downer. Fred (Texas) and I kicked it back and forth for a while. Fred's a conservative let-them-solve-their-own-problems-even-if-they-blow-themselves-to-hell sort of guy. But I like him. He's tough but he listens.

I hoped Vlad (Bosnia) would log in, since he'd had some real experience with international peacekeepers. But he didn't and that made me uneasy. Vlad had been telling us for months about the problems in his country: the threat of renewed civil war; the poverty; the poor sanitation; the closed hospitals; the unexploded artillery shells lying around. Altogether, some pretty nasty stuff. But he hadn't been around in a few days, and I was beginning to have some doubts. Maybe he was just another American kid masquerading as something he wasn't, an American kid who'd had his fun and wandered off to make trouble somewhere else. Still, I wanted to believe in Vlad. And if he was real, I just hoped he was okay.

Suddenly, Sonja (Norway) popped into the middle of an exchange between Fred (Texas) and me.

```
Sonja (Norway): hey kids. i'm here. want hear
news?
```

I sighed and dropped my fingers to the keyboard, figuring I'd better get her under control right from the start. But Fred, who has a lot more patience with distractions than I have, had already begun to type.

Fred (Texas): new pair of skis sonja?

Sonja (Norway): no that is last week news.

Fred (Texas): new boyfriend?

Sonja (Norway): oh they come go. i don't worry.

Fred (Texas): sven's history huh?

Sonja (Norway): no he still here. and erik
and jon.

Jill (Oregon): how many do you keep at once?

Sonja (Norway): i do no count.

Art (Kansas): more than you do jill-babe.

Jill (Oregon): like you know dope.

Art (Kansas): ain't hard to tell these things.

Don (Illinois): come on guys. joel you going
to keep these guys in line?

For some reason, my hands felt almost too heavy to lift.
Finally, I typed:

Joel (Wisconsin): ya come on guys. sonja tell us
your news so we can get back to the question.

Sonja (Norway): what is the big question?

People waited for me, but I just sat. Finally, Fred
answered.

Fred (Texas): international peacekeeping.
what's your news.

Sonja (Norway): i got my belly button pierced.

Art (Kansas): you got your navel pierced? why?

Sonja (Norway): why not? i thought it be fun.

Jill (Oregon): ya why not arty? it's her body.

Art (Kansas): right! then why does she want to poke holes in it.

Fred (Texas): navel or ears. what's the difference?

Art (Kansas): and i imagine tongues are ok too. you pierce your body freddy?

Fred (Texas): nope but it wouldn't be your business if i did.

Kathy (New Brunswick): my mom almost had a bird when i got my ears pierced again. that makes four holes in one ear and three in the other but i figure i got all these earrings why shouldn't i wear them?

Cal (London): i tried orange and green hair for a while. bloody marvelous the looks i got.

Pero (Rome): like the american basketball player? name?

Don (Illinois): dennis rodman. hey good ballplayer. i don't care what color his hair is man.

Pero (Rome): yes very good. not like Michael
Jordan but ok. good tattoos too.

Don (Illinois): wait a second. you're saying
mj isn't good?

Pero (Rome): oh no. very good!

Don (Illinois): ya I thought that was what you
meant. and the rod-mans tattoos are very cool.

I leaned back, hands behind my head, staring at the
ceiling. I was going to shut it down for good. We couldn't
keep our concentration anymore. Here we were: an international teen colloquium on body piercing, hair color, basketball, and tattoos. Just make the announcement and
then give Sonja a parting shot. One she'd remember for a
long time. I tried to imagine how Sonja (Norway) should
look. How Adrien might imagine her.

I dropped my hands to the keyboard, fingers ready to fly,
and stopped. Vlad (Bosnia) had logged into the chat room.

Vlad (Bosnia): hi everyone. sorry i gone
three days. little brother hurt by land mine
expluding. right no foot no leg. other
better. he in hospital. sorry . . . things not
so good hear.

There was a long pause. Finally I typed:

Joel (Wisconsin): hey sorry vlad. hope he
comes thru ok.

The others came in, one by one:

Fred (Texas): ya sorry vlad. thats tough.

Jill (Oregon): say we're thinking of him huh?

Art (Kansas): sorry vlad. lousy land mines. we
ought to talk about them some night joel.

A few more said sorry and then Sonja took her turn.

Sonja (Norway): sorry vlady. really really
sorry. give him our love. and joel i'm sorry i
got everyone talking about navels and stuff.
tell us the big question again.

I've got all sorts of questions for you, I thought. I typed:

Joel (Wisconsin): international peacekeeping.
when is it justified? who should do it? how
much force is ok? you first sonja.

I could almost feel Sonja hesitate. *This is it,* I thought.
Are we going to stay open or not? Make or break is in your hands.
She started in:

Sonja (Norway): i think when many innocent
people are dying then the world has to do
something. if it takes peacekeepers with guns
then maybe thats how it has to be.

Fred (Texas): problem is it always seems like the u.s. sends the troops and foots the bill.

Pero (Rome): italians help sometime. in africa we do much with no help.

Cal (London): and brits too. with iraq lots of countries helped.

Fred (Texas): ya, but that wasn't really peacekeeping. that was kicking saddam's butt so everybody could have oil.

Art (Kansas): lets stick to the question. does peacekeeping work well enough for the cost. and i mean the cost in lives.

Don (Illinois): i say yes. most of the time anyway. i give a rap about those kids caught up in all that crap in yugoslavia and bosnia and those places.

Jill (Oregon): i'm with sonja and don. sometimes we need to do something.

The discussion went on that way to the end, everybody keeping cool and thinking hard. Jill and Art (who I figure are going to look each other up someday and get married) went round and round about the United Nations but didn't lose their tempers. Vlad (Bosnia) typed a long, careful comment on Bosnia and NATO. He apologized about five times for his grammar, but the grammar didn't make any difference. The guy was for real—had been there and was there, God help him.

It was closing time. I leaned forward and typed:

```
Joel (Wisconsin): thanks everybody. have
courage. remember, no fear. sonja meet you
out front in five minutes.
```

I leaned back and smiled when I got the response.

```
Sonja (Norway): ???!!!
```

So I guess the story ends pretty much like it was supposed to. I put my computer to sleep and went out to enjoy the autumn evening. My parents were still arguing in the kitchen, so I left by the front door. Three houses away, Adrien came down from her porch, pulling on a light jacket. She didn't look hugely happy with me.

"Okay, how'd you know?" she snapped.

"Oh, it's a small world." I started walking toward the park, and she followed.

"Come on, Joel. How'd you know?"

"You let on things. A couple of weeks ago you didn't know that the Norwegian hockey team had won an exhibition against the Russians. Real big stuff in Norway. Tonight . . . well, come on. Belly button? What Norwegian kid is going to call it that? Then every time you got serious, you'd forget to leave out words and to mess up your tenses. You sounded just like you."

She looked at me. "How mad are you?"

"Not very. You didn't hurt anything and whenever you got serious you had good stuff to say."

"Well, thanks. I guess . . . It was hard not to be serious after Vlad logged on. I just can't get it out of my head about his little brother getting his leg blown off. I just hate to think there's nothing we can do but talk about land mines some night. There ought to be more."

"I think there are some organizations that work on the issue. We could look into it. They're bound to have Web pages."

"Yeah, but guys like Fred and Art aren't going to go along with raising money for any Princess Diana Fund."

"Hard to say. We'll have to talk about it."

"I guess that's the place to start," she said.

We walked on for a few minutes without saying anything. Gosh, it was an incredible evening, what with the stars out, a moon rising, and all the smells of leaves and autumn and frost in the air. "I've got one question," I said. "Why'd you do it? I thought you hated the chat room."

She shrugged. "Oh, I figured somebody should keep an eye on you."

I laughed. "Why? Did you think I'd get seduced by some babe from the chat room? That I'd run away to meet her in Las Vegas or some place?"

She shrugged again. "Something like that . . . So you guessed all along that I was Sonja Norway, huh?"

"Oh, not all along, but I was pretty sure you were an American after a couple of weeks. The last couple of days I kind of wondered if it was you. Tonight cinched it."

She sighed. "Darn. I really wanted to be Sonja Norway. Tall, blond, athletic. Some Nordic goddess on skis."

"I'll call you Sonja if you like."

"Na, that's okay. I don't really fit the name."

"I like Adrien better, anyway. And I've always liked small and sultry better than tall and blond."

She gave me a skeptical look. "Is that supposed to mean something?"

"Maybe."

"Something about you and me?"

"We could give it a try."

She considered. "I'm not going to compete with your computer. At least not all the time."

"Not a problem. I'm thinking of cutting back the chat room to an hour and a half every other night and letting Fred or Vlad or somebody else do the hosting half the time."

"Why not just end it? Try something new for a change?"

"Do you think we should?"

"Oh, it's *we* now, huh?"

"Well, I'd like to hear your opinion."

She thought for a long minute. "No, I guess we should keep talking."

"That's what I figure," I said, and took a breath because I wasn't sure how this next part was going to sound. "The way I see it, everybody's got to remember that we're all connected. That we're all caught in the same web together."

"Not caught. Part of the same web."

"Yeah, you're right. Part of the same web. And if we remember that and keep talking, then maybe we'll all come through all right. Maybe we'll be able to handle what's coming."

She slipped her arm through mine. "All of us coming through all right," she said. "Yeah, I think we've got to believe that."

And after the chill of cyberspace, her hand was a warm, firm reality in mine.

Alden R. Carter

Alden R. Carter's *Bull Catcher* was an American Library Association Best Book for Young Adults, an ALA Quick Pick for Young Adults, an *American Bookseller* Pick of the Lists, winner of the Arthur Tofte Juvenile Fiction Book Award from the Council for Wisconsin Writers, and winner of the Outstanding Achievement in Children's Literature Award from the Wisconsin Library Association. These are typical of the honors heaped upon his nine novels, twenty nonfiction books, and four picture books. *Sheila's Dying, Growing Season, Up Country, Between a Rock and a Hard Place,* and *Wart, Son of Toad* were all named ALA Best Books for Young Adults. In 1996 *Dogwolf* was an *American Bookseller* Pick of the Lists and appeared on the New York Public Library's Books for the Teen Age list. In addition, the ALA in 1994 named *Up Country* one of the 100 Best of the Best Books for Young Adults published between 1967 and 1992. Carter's most recent book for teenagers is *Crescent Moon,* a historical novel set at the end of the lumbering era in Wisconsin.

Among Carter's award-winning nonfiction books are *The War of 1812: Second Fight for Independence,* winner of an Outstanding Achievement in Children's Literature Award from the Wisconsin Library Association, *The Spanish-American War: Imperial Ambitions,* named Best Juvenile Nonfiction Book of the Year by the Council for Wisconsin Writers, and *China Past—China Future,* also named the Best Juvenile Nonfiction Book of the Year by the Council for

Wisconsin Writers as well as a New York Public Library Book for the Teen Age.

With his nine-year-old daughter, Siri, Alden R. Carter published *I'm Tougher than Asthma,* which won numerous honors, including a Cooperative Children's Book Center Choice and an Orbis Pictus nomination from the National Council of Teachers of English. *Big Brother Dustin,* a picture book about Down syndrome, won an Oppenheim Toy Portfolio Gold Seal Award and was a *Sesame Street Parents* Reviewer's Choice. Carter's most recent picture books are *Seeing Things My Way,* a book about vision impairment, with photographs by his wife, Carol, and *Dustin's Big School Day,* a photoessay sequel to *Big Brother Dustin.*

Carter's "Y2K.CHATRM43," like most of the stories in this book, was written on a computer, and everything related to the publication of this story—including prewriting ideas, revisions, the historical background, and the biographical sketch—was shared between the writer and the editor by e-mail. It is the author's belief that "the Web is binding us together in ways that no previous generation could even imagine. That's a little frightening sometimes," Carter admits, "but I think the Web will help us to talk enough sense to each other that we'll manage to find our way to a more peaceful, healthier world."

For more information about Alden R. Carter, check out his Web site at www.tznet.com/busn/acarterwriter.

ABOUT THE EDITOR

Born just before the outbreak of World War II to an Italian immigrant father and a first-generation Dutch American mother in Paterson, New Jersey, Donald R. Gallo attended high school during the 1950s and graduated from college in 1960. Although he never adopted a hippie lifestyle, he does admit to having worn bell-bottoms and an occasional beaded necklace in the 1970s, which looked a bit strange with his crew-cut hair. But what used to be a crew-cut top is now bald, and he keeps the sides longer and the back in a ponytail.

Having taught nearly thirty years as an English professor, Gallo now spends his time writing and editing books for children, teenagers, and teachers. Among his publications are eight highly praised collections of short stories, including *Sixteen*, which the American Library Association considers one of the 100 Best of the Best Books for Young Adults published between 1967 and 1992, and *No Easy Answers*, an ALA Best Book for Young Adults as well as a Quick Pick for Reluctant Readers. In 1992 Gallo received the ALAN Award for his outstanding contributions to young adult literature.